# DRACONIANS QUEEN

## JUNO WELLS

# CONTENTS

Alien Protector's Rescued Bride is a stand-alone but is part of the Draconian Warrior's Series.

You'll enjoy it more if you start at the beginning!

### *Alien Warrior's Captive Bride*

MANY THOUSANDS OF YEARS AGO, DEEP IN THE EXION star system the first Draconian female entered the cave of ascension. She passed through the softly glowing waters, noticing tiny glowing blobs moving about in the water. Whether they were finless fish or worms was difficult to tell, for they had the characteristics of both as well as thin filaments growing out of their frail bodies.

Knowing the cave must be her divine destiny, the first queen forced herself to submit to the will of the gods. She walked slowly through the glowing waters, emerging a queen on the other side. Her people were equal parts awed and terrified when she disappeared beneath the eerie luminescent liquid, for none had dared to pass through the glowing waters before.

Taking her rightful place as the leader of her people, all was well for a brief time. Soon her sleep became restless. A suspicion crept forward from the back of her mind, even as she felt something strange growing in her body. It moved around and playfully tickled her insides. Since she had no fever, nor evidence of disease upon her skin, horns or wings, the healers assured her that all was well.

Then the nightmares started, and she never knew a moment's peace thereafter. Every day was a struggle to shut out the dark voice growing ever stronger in her mind. Once the symbiont took full control of her faculties, the young woman was forced to stand idly by while the creature wreaked havoc on her people.

From that day to this, every Draconian female had been forced to walk through the waters of ascension, thus becoming a queen in her own right. Those who failed to ascend were killed or sold into slavery. Death was preferable, since Draconian female slaves could look forward to a lifetime of torture by beings furious with their treatment at the hands of the Draconian empire.

A millennia slipped idly by, while the evil of the cave fell into myth. Ascension came to be known as a coming of age ceremony for young females and the Draconians were taught to love this sacred rite, thus perpetuating the age of the symbiont. The first symbiont was long lived and few knew it still wandered the verse looking for plunder and warriors.

As the decades flew by, the queens grew discontented, fought amongst themselves and battled with each other over warriors. They seemed to grow stronger, crave chaos and feed off the misery of others. Little did the Draconians know, but the luminescent creatures floating in the waters of the cave of ascension were not some strange anomaly naturally occurring on their planet, but rather the spawn of a soul sucker that had been driven from a nearby world.

Meanwhile on Earth the environment was deteriorating, turning the oceans into putrid acidic cesspools devoid of all lifeforms. The lives of many males were lost in an effort to clean up the contamination, and then the worst-case scenario came to pass. A new pathogen emerged and locked onto the male genome. It took time to develop an antigen, costing more lives still. By the time all was said and done, the ratio of males to females was seriously unbalanced, there being four females to every male.

Just when humans were losing all hope of survival on their harsh world, aliens made contact with the peoples of Earth. They not only offered to help manage the environmental disaster, but also provided much needed medical supplies and food stuffs. In return, the aliens requested the one thing Earth had a surplus of.

Voluntary human brides were offered in exchange for the supplies. Many women were all too happy to relocate to a pristine new planet with an accommodating alien husband. It beat the alternative, which was living in huge crowded bio-domes.

A large group of human brides were stolen by pirates intent on selling them to the highest bidder. Incompetent fools that they were, they strayed into a spatial anomaly and ended up in Draconian space. Just when their situation seemed hopeless, they were rescued by Draconian warriors. The fight that ensued was one of mythical proportions, resulting in the ship and crew escaping back to normal space.

This is the story of those warriors and the human women they rescued settling a new home world under the protection of the Intergalactic Council of Planets. Unfortunately, the parasitic queen escaped as well. Now the Draconians are always looking over their shoulder, searching for the missing parasite, and do all within their power to ensure the creature does not begin propagating among the human population.

## 1 / ESCAPE
### LATISHA

Rough hands pull me from my tiny darkened room. You'd think that after being kept in such a confining space for the better part of a year I'd be thrilled to be out. I'm not. Part of me is terrified but the larger part is raring for a fight. I'm not stupid, though, so I'm going to bide my time until there is a good chance of making my escape. There's no telling what these aliens have in mind for me. Whatever it is, they're going to be in for a shock when this little earthling gives them the slip.

Glancing up at the super tall male with one hand wrapped around my upper arm, I can't imagine a more nondescript alien. He's tall, thin and milky white with dark eyes and virtually no facial features to describe. His nostrils are mere slits against his upper lip. I've never seen such a small mouth, not even on a newborn baby. I call them talls, cause I'm tired of trying to figure out the real names of all of the strange aliens I meet. None of them speak my language or seem interested in teaching me theirs, so talls it is.

My mind wanders as he literally walks off with me in tow. One has to wonder how talls eat with such tiny mouths. It is possible they absorb nutrients through their skin or inhale it through tubes stuffed into those tiny nostrils. Struggling to keep up with his long legs, I feel his fingers digging into my soft flesh. I seal my lips to keep from groaning, cause most but not all of the aliens I've met don't like it when I make noises or try to talk to them. Maybe the pitch of my voice hurts their ears or they don't like being reminded I exist. It doesn't matter. Being owned by the talls is the best I've had it by far, so I'm not keen to mess that up.

I signed up for the galactic brides program years ago, but never made it to my insanely handsome assigned alien husband. My family probably thinks I'm dead. Instead some kind of crazy space pirates attacked our ship. They were covered in bright yellow fur and walked on all fours barking orders in a language I couldn't understand. After several rounds of sniffing us, they got rid of me and the other women on the ship real quick. It left me with the feeling that we either smelled like last week's garbage to them or they were more interested in having the ship they bested in battle that was carrying us. We all got separated and I've been sold to several species, each stranger than the one before.

I got bought by some rich alien who kept me in a cage and brought me out at parties for everyone to gape at. Being stared at like a zoo animal really sucked. The creep had other aliens, always female, who got staged around the room as well. Since we were all kept in different rooms, I never got a chance to try to communicate with any of them.

Being owned by the rich alien was the bane of my existence because he was the exception on a long list of aliens who didn't like to hear me talk or make noises. He and his guests and staff liked to poke me with padded sticks and laugh when I made a noise. They'd catch me from behind when I wasn't looking or when I was sleeping. The louder my noises, the more they enjoyed the game. They even had contests to see who could get me to cry out the loudest or the most times in a cycle. Eventually, I just forced myself to stop responding. They were really disappointed and sold me to a race of reptilians.

I don't like remembering how awful those guys were. I wasn't with them very long but I heard people screaming the walls down. Their voices were high pitched and squealy, reminding me of something aquatic. My time on their vessel was spent worrying about if and when whatever made the others scream would be visiting that kind of pain and agony on me.

Anyways, one day all the screaming stopped, a tall milky white alien looked through the window of my room on the reptilian ship and all hell broke loose. There was shouting and clanging the likes of which I've never heard. It was ten times louder than the sound of one lone victim screaming in the darkness.

The next thing I knew, I'm being carted off by a large group of talls. They took me to their ship and kept me in the little room for I'm guessing months. They fed me, looked through the little window at intervals, changed out my bedding and sanitized the room every few days. There was a sink to wash up in and a strange alien toilet that made my poop disappear in twinkling lights right after I finished. Though they've been the nicest owners I've had so far, I'm still chafing at being owned and worried about what the talls plan to do with me.

Today, all that waiting came to an end. I'm stumbling to keep up with mister long legs. He looks serious, has a weapon strapped to each hip, and a shiny crystal embedded in his forehead. I can't imagine what it all means but I'm pretty sure I'm not going to like the talls' endgame.

Since I'm not chained up as we navigate the corridors of their ship, I'm already plotting and planning my escape. When we exit the ship, I realize we've landed on a planet. His grip is firm but not bruising. That's when it hits me that they've been treating me real nice and feeding me so I look nice for the auction block. The thing is, I've been there and done that one time too many.

Not being restrained gives me an advantage. One I exploit the moment we're in the crowded marketplace. We must be on a central planet because the place is packed with different species. We stop when my tall gets a message on his communications unit. Finally, luck is on my side.

No sooner does his hand slip from my arm, than I accidentally get slimed by a squid-like alien meandering by. Realizing it bumped into me, the being jerks its tentacle back and leans towards me making a squeaky noise. I believe it to be an apology of some sort.

I smile and murmur politely, "No problem."

Upon seeing my teeth, the alien freezes in place for a brief moment. Feeling devious, I snap my teeth at it and somehow keep from laughing when it runs away in a fright. All its tentacles get tangled up in poor creature's haste to get away from the terrifying human and it almost topples over. I'm a bad woman for doing that but strangely enough feel no remorse. I guess being owned by every species in the galaxy hardens a person.

The tall guy is now shouting angrily into his com unit and I see the moment for what it is, a chance to finally escape. Since the talls have been reasonably nice to me compared to the others, taking a slow walk back away from him seems like breaking up with the best of a long line of creepy boyfriends. Unfortunately, there weren't enough men on earth to have a creepy boyfriend, much less a string of them.

Once I'm ten steps away, I turn and make run for it. Seeing heads turn in my direction, I quickly realize no one else is running, I slow to a brisk walk to avoid drawing more unwanted attention to myself and put as much distance between myself and the tall as possible. I'm short and kind of inconspicuous but being human draws notice. I grab a dark brown cloak that I spy draped over the back of a chair. Since there's no one sitting at the table, I choose to believe the owner left it behind by accident. Wealthy people sometimes get preoccupied and forget items that aren't critical to their existence. Finders, keepers I tell myself.

After being homeless on Earth since I was a tween, grifting comes as naturally to me as breathing. I'm a thief with high moral values, so I never take more than I need, share with those less fortunate than me and never take anything of real worth.

There are thousands of people coming and going in this area. Shuttles are flying overhead, waiting for some of them to take off so they can land. The further away I get from the marketplace, the more apparent it becomes that this planet is a hub of trade for the beings in this sector of space. Relief and happiness war for the top spot in my emotions. This is the kind of place where a girl could easily get lost in the crowd.

It appears to be late afternoon and the suns are setting. There's no way to tell how long it will take the sun to set on this planet. It might take hours or minutes. I'm also concerned about the weather. Although it's dry and arid, the temperature might drop to below freezing at night.

I wander around for hours, trying to figure out a place to

bed down. Eventually, I find a mammoth building with a flat roof. Since part of it is obscured by trees, it's unlikely shuttles flying overhead will see me. I'll just have to sleep wrapped in my stolen cloak for the night and hope for the best. My stomach is growling and my throat is parched. Hunger and thirst are not strangers to me, so I grin and bear it. At least I'm free. That gives me solace as I try to figure out how to survive on a world where no one speaks my language and I'm actively being hunted.

I'm certain there's a bounty on my head. When I was sneaking around the city earlier, I saw huge monitors in the marketplace and financial districts flashing my face, among other things. Below my image was a three-digit number, or what looked like a number. It flashed brightly for a few seconds and then other images played across the screen. It reminded me of the electronic billboards on Earth. Since everyone's seen my face, I can't show it in this city. Maybe if I lay low, they'll give up after a while.

Snuggling down into a shaded corner of the building, I try to rest. Just when I'm dozing off I sense movement from the far side of the building and something makes a deep guttural sound from the darkness. The sound doesn't sound like it came from a person. Something inside me breaks to know I've managed to get free only to be torn to pieces by some wild animal.

A huge paw steps out into the moonlight, a paw with claws and dirty green molted fur attached to a muscular arm. I press myself back as far as I can, feeling the metal building press uncomfortably into my spine. The creature slowly stalks forward and I see green eyes, long fangs and a bulging belly that slowly moving in a way that communicates she's pregnant rather than just panting.

She moves lightning quick, and before I can even

scream, she's swatted me to the side and pressed me onto my back with her claw on my throat. Her claws flex as if she's daring me to scream. Maybe I'm imagining that part but staring into her eyes I see an otherworldly intelligence reflected back at me.

My hands wrap instinctively around her arm as I try to pry her off me. She makes that menacing noise again and I freeze. Her paw moves to the side and she stands on my hair. A huge head comes down to my neck, and just when I think she's going to tear my throat out, she inhales. I'm too startled to react. She's inhaling over and over again in different places along my neck and face.

Her nose moves over and she licks the fingernail that's still clinging to her arm. It seems as though the big feline is trying to figure out if they're sharp. I hold still and let her sniff me, remembering that domesticated animals on Earth inhale a person's scent in an effort to get to know them. I think she's domesticated because she's wearing a collar.

Her nose moves over my torso and she pokes her snout between my legs, noses around. I snap back to reality in an instant and back up, shoving her away. When my stomach rumbles loudly, she backs up and begins making noises again. They're not growls or purrs, but they don't remind me of any kind of speech I've encountered in my travels.

She's determined that I'm no threat. I can tell because she turned her back on me and that's not something you do if you think the stranger you just met poses any kind of danger.

When she moves away, it's on all fours yet she's not moving quite like an animal either. Her legs are double jointed and she's kind of walking like a person only hunched over and using her hands for balance. I'm now more fascinated than scared because she's moving to the far side of the building again. I watch her leap from the building and push off a nearby tree before she hits the ground with a soft thud. I don't know if she left or not. My hearing is simply not good enough to pick up her prowling on the ground.

I let out one shaky breath after another. That's one of the stranger experiences I've had with an alien. I'm still going back and forth in my mind trying to figure out if she's an alien or an animal. Well, naturally she's an alien, regardless of whether she's humanoid or not. I clarify in my own drowsy mind that I mean to say I don't know for sure if she's sentient or not. One thing is for certain, she can move pretty stealthily and fast to be carrying a litter of whatever's in her distended stomach.

Although I try to stay awake and alert to unforeseen dangers, I keep nodding off. My dreams are filled with being trapped in a cage. Hunger gnaws at my insides and the cold metal floor absorbs what little natural body heat I have. Terrifying noises come from the darkness surrounding my cage. I feel small, alone and unwanted. Suddenly, sticks are being poked through the bars, jabbing me in the sides, stomach and legs. I seal my lips because I know this game. They're trying to see which one of them can startle me and make me scream. Refusing to play their game is the only way to win.

Something damp and smelly smacks my face and my eyes shoot open. I see the feline from last night staring down at me. She's dripping wet and breathing heavily. I struggle to sit up and she moves back. Something round and red hits me in the leg, and for a brief moment, I think she wants to play ball. Then I realize it's a baseball-sized fruit of some kind. When I scan the area, I discover a pile of them. No wonder she's panting. I can't imagine how or why but it appears she brought me food.

I pick it up and test the weight of it in my hand before smelling it. Taking a moment to wipe it on my clothes, I sniff it again, enjoying the sweet aroma. It definitely smells as good as it looks.

The feline grumbles something and then just throws her head down and chomps into the one she just put between her paws. As she's eating, I notice they aren't paws exactly. She has three short stubby fingers and a flap that could act as a thumb. Her maw opens so wide that she's making very little mess. After just a few bites the entire fruit is gone.

Since it feels a bit like a plum, I bite into it. It is sweet, juicy, and although I should feel sick after eating such a sweet fruit on an empty stomach, I feel almost instantly amazing. The more I eat, the better I feel. The fruit is so juicy that my thirst is being quenched.

I smile and point to the fruit. "You, my scruffy friend, are a lifesaver." I dip my head in appreciation like I have seen some aliens do. I'm having a hard time dialing down my enthusiasm. "I don't know where you found these but it's the best thing I've tasted since leaving Earth. Thank you."

She says something I can't understand and rolls another piece of her bounty my way. We sit eating until I can't hold another bite. She noses one over into the corner where I slept for later and wanders off. I sit back, watching the sun crest over the city. Maybe if I can get out of the city, I can survive on the natural vegetation. I don't know anything about this planet so that's a huge hindrance. For all I know there could be predatory animals or poisonous plants that look edible.

I'm not counting on my mangy new friend to save the day again. I can't believe she's able to jump onto this building with that huge stomach of hers. Grabbing the last piece of fruit, I roll it between my hands. For now I'm feeling okay. I just need to stay sharp, keep my head covered and hope they give up searching for me soon.

## 2 /  NEW DUTY ASSIGNMENT
### KANE

STROLLING INTO THE LOADING BAY, I CAN HARDLY throttle back my excitement. Today I join the esteemed ranks of warriors. My crisp new uniform is nothing like the soft clothing our young warriors wear for schooling. The hard plating will protect me in battle and the suit has an environmental system built in. It's designed to protect me in case I'm vented into space. After twenty-five solar cycles surviving the rule of draconian queens, I pray to the goddess that nothing that horrid ever happens to me.

I imagine being vented into orbit around our new Draconian home world and suffering the indignity of floating endlessly around the planet while other warriors reference me as a sad example of what happens to new warriors who do not follow proper safety protocols. The thought sends a chill creeping up my spine.

My father has been nice enough to take me under his wing and train me in the ways of being a warrior, though he is new to the ranks himself. I cannot shame him by making foolish or embarrassing mistakes. He has been through much hardship in his life, so I have no wish for him to lose a favored son or be the butt of jokes by other warriors over my ineptitude.

I catch his eye from across the bay and he motions me to his side. Moving quickly, I can see my reflection in all the shiny metal fighters as I walk through the bay. I have no battle scars yet, but with luck I will see my first battle soon. Instead of making dull trade runs, I hope to be assigned where the action is. Looking longingly at the sleek modern fighters, I dream of piloting one in a glorious battle in protection of our new human queens. They are small, delicate creatures with big hearts. I will see no harm come to them after they've risked their own lives to help us secure our freedom from the rule of ruthless draconian queens.

As I approach, I see my father is now working on a fighter. By the time I reach him he's laid on his back with the upper part of his body under the main manifold. I squat down and peer under the fighter. "Greetings, father." I use the human term instead of sire out of deference to our new human queens. I am not the only warrior infatuated with them, so there is no shame in honoring them in any way we can.

My sire slides out from under the fighter and peers up at me, wiping a large wrench with a cleaning cloth. Like me, he's huge and muscular. His blue skin is marked with the symbols of our clade. His wings are spread out beneath him to take the weight off his wing base while he works. "Greetings, my scion. Welcome to the ranks of warriors." Coming to his feet, he gazes into my eyes when I rise to stand before him. "You have it in you to be a strong protector. You must be alert to danger, train hard and pay attention to details, for your life depends upon recognizing danger and determining the most effective way to neutralize it. Warriors are not mindless fighting machines, so do not think to rely upon your muscles when leveraging your brain would better serve your purpose."

Swallowing thickly, I dip my head respectfully and tighten my wings behind me. If he is gifting me with an oration, this is a more solemn occasion than I first thought. My sire has thoughtfully chosen words of wisdom to suit the moment. "I will not allow mindless battle lust to rule my actions, father." That's always a possibility with younger warriors, so he's right to caution me in that regard.

The corners of his mouth turn up. "You will be pleased with your first assignment. I have arranged for you to join a trade party with three other novice warriors to Brackon Five. Your mission is to procure extra backup parts for the ship we recently acquired in battle. Your efforts will keep the ship operational when we are no longer near trade planets."

I can't help but frown up at him. "We're tasked with scavenging spare parts for the ship?" There's no glory to be had in an assignment like that, thus the disappointment churning in my gut.

My sire's voice becomes more serious. "Don't take any assignment lightly, especially not this one. If we do not acquire those parts, the ship won't continue to be the kind of environment we've come to expect and it certainly won't be appropriate for a queen."

Nodding, I lift my wings. We must protect our new queens at all costs. "We'll get everything on the list, even if we have to resort to having them fabricated."

"That's the attitude I like to see in my eldest son. Brackon Five is a sparsely populated planet whose primary economy is driven by trade with other worlds. It's well policed, so we don't expect your team to run into any problems other than the tedious job of tracking down the parts we need."

"I will not fail you, father. I am honored by your trust in me."

"Our needs are many so it is likely the four of you will on the planet for a few cycles."

"I will keep my focus on the mission."

Taking a deep breath, he jerks his chin towards the com device on my shoulder. "There should be time enough for you enjoy yourself if you work efficiently. There are many traders on Brackon Five. Though you are newly inducted into the ranks of warriors, it is never too early to begin preparing for your future. I have placed credits into your account. Spend them wisely with an eye towards building a nest for your queen."

Now I'm totally lost. "I have no queen, father." What I don't say is that it's unlikely I ever will, since females are few and precious. I'm a low-ranking warrior and can't imagine a queen selecting me as a breeding partner." No sooner do the words form in my own mind than I realize that I am the son of a breeder. Therefore, I am at risk of being selected. He must see the understanding cross my face because he says no more on the subject. His hand comes out to land on my shoulder. "Coming of age among our kind results in many responsibilities being thrust upon you all at once. You are ready to face them."

The silence spins out between us and I straighten, readying myself for whatever comes my way. "I can do this," I murmur under my breath.

"Yes, you can. Now, go to the armory and gear up. The scavenging team is awaiting your arrival."

I hustle to the armory as quickly as my legs will carry me, lest I get left behind or be thought irresponsible. The moment I step into the room, I see that instead of three warriors, there is only one.

Though he is large, he's not quite as large as me. Trying not to preen, I wait for his orders. His skin is green with dark brown shades tipping his scales. Massive wings are tucked neatly behind his back, as is his tail. Black horns spiral up from his cranial ridge on each side of his head. Such is the way with alphas. His dark eyes look me over as if assessing my battle readiness. I remain frozen in place, not wishing to be found lacking by my superior officer. Though he's not much older than me, it's clear he's in charge because he's wearing the lowest level commander's stripe along the collar of his uniform.

When his eyes find mine again, I realize he's waiting for me to present myself to him. Lifting my wings, I state formally, "Greetings, Commander Hatch."

He turns slightly and one hand comes out to slam shut his personal locker. There is a bank of them along the wall, reserved for officers only. When he turns back to me, his expression is curious. He's not nearly as large or impressive as I am, with his bland green coloring and sinewy wings. I'm still envious because he has something I don't. That something is rank. He's earned it by proving himself to be honorable, diligent and hardworking. I snap to attention when he speaks. "And you are?"

Shoving aside my embarrassment at not introducing myself properly, I sound off. "I'm Kane of the house of Dreck." Dipping my head, I stammer, "Reporting for duty on the away team, sir."

There is a tiny shake of his head and he doesn't even attempt to conceal his exasperation. "They sent me a breeder? Can you even fight?"

"Of course, sir. I completed all my training modules successfully."

The other male's expression clears. "I'd heard they were opening the training to breeders and females."

"I didn't see any queens during my time in the training pits." A frown creases my ridge, as I try to imagine a queen training to become a warrior. The humans are so small and fragile. I don't think training them to fight is such a good idea.

A cold voice sounds off from the doorway. "He's lucky to be here at all. Breeders joining the ranks of warriors is something I never thought to see in my lifetime."

"Close your mouth, Drac. If he finished his training, he's earned his spot." Unlike Hatch, Drac is huge. His wing-span must be massive. His bloodline is pure warrior. I can tell by the drab grey, brown and black coloration of his scales. It's natural camouflage, shifting colors slightly to enable him to blend into any environment. His horns wrap back against his head, presumably an evolutionary advantage to keep him from casting an identifiable silhouette. Standing there, gazing at him, I know real envy for the first time.

Drac rubs his chin thoughtfully. "He's weak. I'm glad this is just a scavenging mission."

My scales itch with embarrassment. We all understand what he's not saying. He doesn't want me watching his back. Warriors have never trusted breeders. In the before times when we were subjugated by Draconian queens, the warriors accused us of being spies, reasoning that if we shared their beds then we shared their confidences. Unfortunately, some breeders let secrets slip. Warriors were severely punished and some lost their lives when minor indiscretions were reported.

Rather than trying to convince them of my trustworthiness, I stick to the facts. "I've been training for almost a solar cycle." Lifting my chin, I speak. "I am the top marksman in my class and excel at hand to hand combat." What I don't say is that I've trained longer and harder than anyone in my training group to gain those rankings.

Hatch murmurs respectfully, "Impressive credentials, for a breeder."

"We're all just warriors now, sir. I'm ready to defend our queens and willing to sacrifice my life if need be."

Another voice joins the mix. "Hold up, hero, this is a low-level parts retrieval mission, not a glorious battle." The newcomer's wings shake with humor as he strolls to his locker. This new team member is one of the smallest warriors I've ever seen. He's so tiny that I make two of him. He's light on his feet and practically glides across the floor on wings so light and delicate, I question if he is one of our adolescent queens. My mouth falls open but I don't speak the words whirling around in my head. Because of course he's a warrior. He has stark green and black scales, the pattern basic. When he begins pulling out medical kits, I realize that he's our medic. Those delicate hands probably enable him to suture wounds and perform delicate surgery with deftness and precision.

Commander Hatch gives the younger warrior a quick disapproving glance before addressing me. "Welcome, Kane from the house of Dreck. Don't pay any attention to Jax. This is an important mission."

Looking from one to the other, all the pieces begin to fall into place. Unlike the others, Drac's a little older than us. If I'm not terribly mistaken Hatch might be in charge but Drac's clearly our child minder on this assignment. Jax is our medic. Though I'd love to be a fighter pilot, I'm clearly the grunt, since I haven't been around long enough to have developed a specialty. Warriors have to prove themselves competent fighters before being allowed to specialize.

"I am pleased to meet each of you and looking forward to completing our mission."

My voice sounds stilted even to my own ears. Drac flicks a wing dismissively in my direction. Jax laughs and Hatch grunts as he loads down his form with far too many weapons for such a mundane mission. I open the locker in front of me and begin gearing up as the others chatter. I have no value to this team until I've proven myself.

We continue to talk as we head for our shuttle. The others are teasing each other and I'm enjoying their casual familiarity. When I catch Hatch's eye, I murmur, "Thank you for accepting me on this mission, commander. I will endeavor to meet your expectations."

He shrugs noncommittally. "Space vessels need fresh parts to fly and our job is to track them down today." Looking none too thrilled to be scavenging parts, he grumbles, "With any luck we'll be finished and throwing back a cool beverage by the time the sun sets."

"I'm happy to be off the ship and doing something that will ensure our survival." My reply is met with a wry chuckle.

We climb aboard the shuttle and Hatch begins performing the pre-flight checks. He grins at me and jerks his chin. "Buckle up, newbie. We can't risk losing a breeder on his very first day of active duty."

His teasing is meant to be light but it stings, nonetheless. I can't help my dry response. "Human queens care nothing for breeders. We're all just males to their eyes."

The others chuckle because it's true.

Dropping down into a seat, I jerk at my safety harness.

"Does everyone in the armada know this is my first day on the job?"

Suddenly everyone is laughing even more. Jax tosses me a smirk. "This is honestly your first day as a warrior?"

I know they aren't going to let this go lightly, so I give them the little speech I prepared for such occasions. "Though I was born and raised on a Draconian military vessel, I have never been permitted to mix among the warriors until this day. My place was at my father's side, learning the ways of being a breeder. Being in the service of our new human queens is an honor, for breeding is no longer a primary designation for ones such as me. Though in the before times each male was either a breeder or a warrior, the human queens breed indiscriminately with whoever strikes their fancy. Since you're as likely to be selected by one of them as me, to my mind that means I should no longer be designated as a breeder." The humor dies away after my grand speech and they stare at me for a long moment.

Drac's voice fills the void. "It is illogical to seek out the lesser status."

I turn to Drac but before I can speak Jax leans forward, capturing my attention. He wrinkles his nose, genuinely perplexed. "You're a breeder and allowed to move freely through the chambers of queens. Why would you give that up to hunt machine parts on a barren world?"

They truly can't get their heads around this issue. "After watching my father suffer under the claw of a Draconian queen, I have no desire to be selected so young in my life." What I keep carefully hidden is that I crave action and adventure, even over the soft touches of our new human queens. I have no wish for them to see me as young, imma-ture and lusting for battle, for that is not seemly for a warrior. We are supposed to fight only when there is no other recourse.

Jax wrinkles his nose, genuinely perplexed. "You are a breeder and allowed to walk among queens."

"It matters not if I walk among them. Human queens have so many vying for their attention that I will never capture their notice. They breed warriors more so than breeders these days. Though one day I may be pressed into service by a queen, today I plan to enjoy all the freedoms that were denied to me in the before times. I will see strange new worlds, meet new species and stand between danger and our queens."

Drac barks a hoarse laugh. "Don't expect to find a glorious battle on this safe and well-guarded planet."

Dipping my head slightly in respect, I try to keep the enthusiasm out of my voice when I reply. "I have never set foot on a planet before. If you find me staring, pinch me." Lifting a brow, I continue, "However, I will eventually have a battle and the chance to distinguish myself."

The mood lightens and they chuckle at my bold words. I don't know whether to be offended or glad they no longer see me as status conscious. In truth, they all seem more amused than annoyed that I'm on their team. That's a huge relief.

Jax drops down in the seat beside me and buckles in as the shuttle takes off. "You're a warrior at heart, my friend. We all wish for the same things."

Hatch looks over his shoulder at me from the navigational console. "We do not go seeking conflict but will meet it head-on if fighting becomes necessary." Leave it to our fearless leader to verbalize the official stance on violence. His firmly spoken words light a fire in my gut. When I look around, the others are all nodding their agreement. I feel accepted and like we are all of a similar mind. Their faces are alight with the same excitement I feel strumming through my own chest. We're a team of four Draconian warriors, all intent on proving the trust our superiors showed us was not misplaced.

## 3 / DRAGON WARRIORS
### LATISHA

CRAWLING ALONG THE SHELF OF A REFUSE TUNNEL, I realize how good I've got it. On Earth this tunnel would have contained raw sewage. However, on Brackon Five all the sewage is treated in individual buildings before being pumped out for yet another treatment. It seems a bit inefficient to me, but what do I know about sewage management on an alien world. I'm just happy to be damp from potable water rather than actual sewage. Each tunnel is about six feet in diameter and has a two-foot ledge built into either side. Again, I have no idea why that is.

A soft guttural noise sounds from in front of me. I'm certain that's my new friend, Lady. I know that naming her was kind of shitty, since she's clearly a sentient being. We tried the whole telling each other our names thing but it didn't work out. My name came out Lish and her name requires some sounds the human throat can't make. I know not everything is a competition but I feel bad because she can at least ballpark my name and I've got zip for hers.

Anyways, we've stuck together for the last three months or so. She brings me food from the forest and warns me of danger. I sneak around, helping her perform odd jobs under the table to buy the things we need to survive. Picking up my pace, I try not to fall off the ledge and into the water. Lady's always got a good reason for what she does and I don't want to be caught in the tunnels if it's time to flush them out or anything like that.

We make it out into the moonlight and rest against the side of a large mound of sandy soil. I see some tree-like things silhouetted against the sky and some plants are growing nearby, but everything seems to be surviving without much moisture. It's all brown, black and purple, giving the appearance of being half dead.

Opening our bag, I pull out a small container and toss Lady a hydration pellet, then put one into my own mouth. The thin membrane dissolves and there's a gush of moisture in my mouth. It's some kind of advanced liquid that hydrates you in under a minute. Even on this arid planet, my thirst is quenched for hours after taking one.

Lady still has her tongue hanging out, so I toss her another pellet. Her pregnancy is proceeding slowly and dehydration is too much of a risk in this environment. Her stomach is bigger than ever. I thought she was about to give birth when I first met her. I guess that I was basing that on the size of her stomach but she's slowly swelled to the point that she looks like she's about to pop. Goodness only knows how long her species carries their young. I just want to keep her as healthy as possible. It's the right thing to do. Besides, we're a team. The twin moons are full and beautiful as I gaze up at them and make a wish that we both survive and somehow make a life for ourselves.

The talls are still looking for me. I still see my image on the view screens in the marketplace from time to time, with ever larger amounts of bounty flashing below. That means showing my face is still not an option.

I've shoveled animal food and separated refuse right alongside Lady. On the upside, I can now operate an alien laundry machine like a pro. Since I don't speak any alien languages, she negotiates with the locals and we both work the jobs. We stick to the couple of species that are really anti whoever is running this planet. They'll hire us, and my best guess from watching them is that they're not cooperative enough with the authorities to turn me in, even for credits. Their defiance is my saving grace in this situation.

These menial jobs put food in our bellies and kept us hydrated but we have to be creative about finding a place to sleep. There are several local mines, but others like us sleep there and I can't risk anyone recognizing me. Whatever reward they're offering for me would set some homeless person's life right again, I'm certain of that.

The downside is sometimes our sketchy employers get curious about what's behind the wrap I wear around my face. We had to take extreme measures to give my last employer the slip. He was getting a little handsy, and since he's got eight of them, it was just a matter of time before he got my face and other miscellaneous body parts uncovered. Figuring out my identity would have put him squarely in control and I can't risk that.

We've migrated to the far side of the city looking for work and a safe place to sleep, desperate and chancing the more dilapidated neighborhoods. I can see the tarmac in the distance and know the huge marketplace is about a three hour walk on the other side of it. Shuttles carrying goods land and lift off all day and into the night. I don't think the trading center ever really closes.

After a short rest, we continue our journey, arriving at

the center of the city just after sunrise. It's dusty and just beginning to fill up with people. Reaching my hand into my cloak, I feel seven chits floating freely in the bottom of my long pocket. It's enough to buy food and water for five or six days. It's not nearly enough because Lady is going to give birth very soon and I have no idea how that's going to go when she can no longer negotiate for work on our behalf.

Lady and I are not the same status on this planet. She's homeless and destitute but has the protection of the law so no one can bother her. Humans are considered property and I've got a bounty on my head. I've been accompanying her on jobs and doing the bits that take opposable thumbs. She got a non-bendable flap for a thumb and it makes doing certain things hard. We're a good team that way. Once she goes into labor, neither of us will be able to work.

I head over to a drink stand while Lady interacts with another vendor. Looking over my shoulder to keep her in my sights, I accidentally stumble into something. Huge claw-tipped fingers come out around my shoulders to stabilize me and when I look up the sun is blocked out by huge wings. It's a male, a huge one. He's got purple and blue scales, horns and really sharp teeth. He shakes me and then shakes me again. I realize his mouth is moving but I only hear disjointed noises. Though it doesn't seem like speech, I know it is. What else could it be after all?

My wrap slips down and he catches a glimpse of my human lips. His eyes get huge and his hands fly off me at the speed of light. The next thing I know he's on one knee with his head bent. Yanking up my hood, I realize everyone is starting to stare. Before I can get away, Lady lands on the ground between us and her soft guttural noise causes the winged man to jerk his head up. She swipes at him with one hand, her claws extended.

Then we're running from the area as quickly as our legs will carry us. I spare a glance over my shoulder to see if he's following and the purple guy's just gaping at us like he's never seen a filthy human and whatever Lady is before. His eyes are a brilliant purple and his wings are unfurled behind him, giving him a majestic appearance. He reminds me of the old Earth myths about dragons in human form.

Lady jumps in front of me like she's prone to do when she sees something I don't. She begins clawing at a metal grate low on the side of a building. It pops off into her hands before I can get to her. She shoves me inside and follows, crowding me, and I move back even more to make room for her. Her three fingered hands grab the grate, tilt it outside the hole and yank it back into place. It's dark inside this hole but we're out of sight and safe.

Lady flops down on her side and curls up, panting. Worried that it might be a thirsty pant, I pull out a hydration tablet for her. "Where are we?" I usually talk to Lady although I'm fairly certain she can't understand me.

She watches me looking around curiously and makes an exasperated noise before reaching towards the grate. There's a small area on the floor where the sunlight is showing through. She begins making a design in the dust there. Moving closer, it looks like she's drawing a building, but then I realize it's two towers with a thick line joining them. She draws a few rudimentary stick figures with one claw, literally scratching the markings into the metal floor.

"It's a bridge," I say excitedly. She shushes me and my hand flies to my mouth.

Now that my eyes have adjusted I inspect our surroundings. We're in a small metal cube, about ten foot squared with a ceiling height of about half that. I can't stand up comfortably, so I elect to set. Giving myself a few moments to calm down, I begin planning what to do next.

My planning is interrupted by intrusive thoughts of the big dragon guy. He wasn't giant huge but he was head and shoulders taller than me. His wingspan must have been close to eighteen feet from tip to tip. I remember his large, expressive eyes crawling all over me before he dropped to his knee. Why he would do something like that is beyond my ability to reason.

Chewing on my bottom lip, I have to admit that although his size was intimidating, he didn't terrify me. I was scared because he was drawing attention to me. I'm conflicted about him. Best thing to do would be to avoid him. The easiest way to do that is just to sit tight. He didn't look like the locals, so chances are he's a trader. Most traders take care of business and leave within a day.

Whatever I am, I'm clearly an inept warrior because the little human queen and her friend queen gave me the slip before I could make her understand that I am a protector of queens. Like the gigantic fool that I am, I just stood there with my mouth hanging open when she clearly needed me to ease her way. Guilt gnaws at my gut as I hustle around looking for the pair of lost souls.

I've never seen a queen so thin and starved as this human. The Sonarian was clearly with child. And I let them run right off without a protector. Tucking my tail between my legs, I head back to the shuttle emptyhanded.

Hatch and the others are sorting and packing their finds when I come running onto the tarmac. His face creases into a frown. "You dare to come back without one single part?"

"Forget parts," I pant. "I stumbled upon two desperate queens."

Everyone drops what they are doing to come to my side. Sucking in air, I try to explain. "I bumped into a human queen wearing rags. I believe she was destitute. She had another female with her. The second queen was Sonarian and heavy with child."

Everyone begins closing the crates and shoving them inside the cargo holds along the bottom of the shuttle. Hatch asks, "Where did they go? We must find them."

Finally catching my breath, I help stow our supplies as I answer. "They disappeared into the crowd. Perhaps the authorities can assist us in locating them."

Pulling out his handheld, Hatch begins the tedious process of contacting the appropriate authority. When we realize he's getting bounced from one civil servant to another, we all jump on our communications devices to assist him in his quest.

Jax is the first to get a hit. "I've found something." We open the link he sends and her face comes up.

"That's her I think. I only saw her lips and her eyes but I suspect she is a shadow of her former self. Her form was slight, even for a human queen. It made me think she was not eating enough."

Hatch responds tightly, "She's been on the run for the better part of two lunars, so I'm not surprised to hear that she's not doing well."

The older warrior, Drac, straightens. "We must find them both. Sonarians do not birth without medical support."

Relief surges through me that they're all on board with locating the failing queens. "I agree. Neither can survive on this planet without warriors to cover them."

Hatch scrolls for a few more seconds before looking up. "The human queen was intended to be a bride for a Storovian who has quit his claim after she was abducted several solars ago. She's been sighted several times, most recently by an Arobian peacekeeper. He took possession of her and contacted Earth authorities who arranged for her to be returned to her home world. Unfortunately, the peace-keeper has not been able to locate her."

I swallow thickly. "She didn't understand my words. That alone tells me she has not been given a translation chip."

"She might have been chipped years ago, before our kind entered the Naxis."

Hatch scrolls through his handheld again and growls. "She was never chipped. Their vessel was carrying a hundred queens and was raided before they could process them all. The peacekeeper was taking her to a medical unit to have the chip inserted when she absconded."

Shock rolls through my body. "She may not know the peacekeeper's goal was to return her to her people."

Snapping his handheld shut, Hatch steps forward. "I agree. The human queen needs to be covered by proper warriors, as does her Sonarian friend. We need to separate and track them down." Looking up at the sky, he continues, "Hunting them down and ensuring their safety is our primary concern. Nothing else matters right now. We rendezvous back here at sunset." Looking at each of us in turn, he adds, "If any of you pick up their scent, sound off on the com. We'll converge on your location."

We immediately disband, each taking a different direc-tion. We're well trained on working in a grid formation. I carefully look over every booth in my designated area, looking for tracks, scenting anything I think they might have touched and maintain high alert for any conflicts that break out. I have no wish for someone to find them before we do, particularly if that person has nefarious intentions. The sun beats down against my shoulders and I spread my wings slightly to block it out. The hot desert environment is no impediment to my mission. Being united in a common cause with these warrior feels more right than anything I've ever known.

## 5 / TRACKING SKILLS
### DRAC

I'M A WARRIOR WITH ONLY ONE THING ON HIS MIND and that is rescuing the two needy queens. It inflames my soul that they've been enslaved, mistreated and starved on this alien world. I blame the males tasked with ensuring her safety, for each and every one of them has let her down. Thanks be to the gods the Sonarian has decided to become her benefactor. If not for that, the human queen would have perished long ago.

When we came to this new sector of space and met the human queens, my mind and my heart softened to them. Though our species is long lived, I am twice the age of the other males on my team. Therefore, it is incumbent upon me to secure the safety of these two queens.

As I move through the settlement, venders call out to me and friendly aliens issue me greetings. Since I have no time for such social niceties, I activate my natural camouflage and weave stealthy through the throng of beings. Being an excellent hunter and having taken the liberty of scenting all the human females aboard our ship, I'm able to pick up her delicious scent. It's faint and tainted with the filth of her living conditions, but I follow it.

What I find leaves me stunned. Deep inside one of the square pillars holding up a moving people carrier, I find them both hidden away. Ripping off the grate, I peer inside, ignoring the stink that assails my nostrils. The human queen jumps back. I've frightened her and it causes me to cringe. Her sweat covered face, stringy dull hair and the threadbare clothing clinging to her bony form evidence the severity of her neglect.

The Sonarian whines and I see the side of her stomach contract. She appears to be in heavy labor but that doesn't keep her from swiping at me with her claws. I stick my head and shoulders into the small space. "I wish you no harm, Sonarian queen. Will you allow me to take you to our healers?"

"Leave us in peace. We have no credits and nothing of value to pay for your medical services." Her voice sounds harsh but my translator understands her every word.

"Our people do not charge for such services. Let me see you properly cared for this night, if not for yourself, then for the unborn you now labor to bring into this world."

Her head comes up to stare at me. "If you attempt to take my young, I will slit your throat, dragon warrior."

Swallowing hard, I nod. "My name is Drac and you can trust my words."

"My name is Trovena. I thank you for your offer of assistance."

"Tell the human to come as well. We have more of her kind on our vessel."

"She will not come. I have tried to talk her into using one of the public communications arrays to contact her home world but she will not. She must have been exiled from her world, for our conditions have been harsh and she would not relent about contacting them."

"Neither you nor the human queen will be forced to return to your home worlds or do any other thing you do not wish. This is my promise to you."

She lifts her arms and I slide my hands underneath her body and lift as carefully as I can. The pregnant Sonarian queen is light in my arms. My throat tightens to know I am lifting a queen in active labor. I can feel her unborn moving in her stomach when I cradle her against my chest. I'm humbled to be the one rescuing her this day. Though we are not breed compatible, I cherish this queen and her babes as though they were my own.

I hold her in my lap, laying her head in the crook of my arm. Her legs dangle over the side of mine and the small cry of pain reminds me that she labors to birth her young. I hesitate to lay her upon the barren ground but holding her at this most auspicious time seems wrong as well.

Feeling like the fool that I am, I pull out my handheld with my free hand and alert the rest of my team that I have found them. Their excited growls fade as I slip the unit back into its cradle at my waist. Draconians are fast. They'll fly to meet us no doubt.

I remember after a few moments that the human queen is here as well. I call out to her, "Human queen, you are rescued by the Draconians. Come forth and know that you are safe under our wing."

She does not emerge, nor do I see a shadow of a movement from within the darkened hole. I worry for the frightened human and for the precious queen in my arms. Both are vulnerable and I have not the words to reassure them. Our newest team member is a breeder. He would know what to say to sooth their battered souls. Glancing up at the sky, I see the sun is setting. My chest expands and I pray fervently for help to arrive quickly.

No sooner do I think the thought than Kane touches gently down beside me. He reaches out to touch the Sonarian's forehead, then his fingers drift down to her neck. "She is not well, Drac. Her breathing is shallow and she does not rouse at the sight of a stranger like her kind are wont to do."

"I'm certain Hatch called for emergency transport." My voice sounds wooden and hollow even to my own ears. I don't know for certain that emergency transport is on its way, but saying the words makes me believe it to be true. I've never feared for my own wellbeing like I fear now for these fragile queens. My hand trembles as I reach up to stroke the Sonarian's shoulder. Her glassy eyes open and they seem unfocused and confused. *Hurry, Jax, we need a medic,* I tell myself. I've seen my team member save lives I didn't think could be saved. He's sure to know what to do with a simple birth.

Within moments Hatch and Jax alight on the ground behind us. I can tell that it's them because I recognize the shape of the shadow their wings cast upon the ground. Jax clamors to our side and flips open his medical kit. I open the arm keeping him from rendering medical care and he moves closer. "Can you help her...save her young?"

"I'm trained in all birthing procedures, but I've never assisted a Sonarian."

Jax is smart and capable. I choose to believe he can help. He pulls out a scanner and begins scanning her stomach area. I am educated, so I know beings do not carry young in their actual stomachs, but right now I am not thinking straight. Though I've never felt anxious, even in the heat of battle, I'm panicking now. My heart is double pumping and my chest feels too small to accommodate the extra blood.

Warriors were not meant for days like this. We are meant to rip our enemies apart in battle, return bloodied and broken long enough to heal for another battle. We aren't supposed to feel emotions such as this. It weakens us.

Over Jax's shoulder I see Hatch peer into the gaping hole where the human queen should be. He turns and I know what he's going to say before the words come out of his mouth. "The space is empty. There is only one way out, so she must have slipped away while you cared for her friend queen."

Will this horrible day never end? Just when I think my mission is complete, it is discovered that we are only half finished. Being so preoccupied with the sickly Sonarian, I allowed the human to escape. I curse that today there is only one of me, when two was needed.

I'm gripping the Sonarian so firmly that I didn't realize my skin was changing color to match hers. Taking a deep breath, I force my camouflage to cease. My chest aches and I do not know exactly why I am reacting so strongly to these vulnerable queens. Perhaps it is because I worry for her and her young or because the human is still in danger. Perhaps it is merely because I wish this mission to be over, so I can crawl into my bed and dream of the lovely face I saw in the wanted bulletin. I will never find another peaceful rest until I am certain the human queen is ensconced safely in our ship.

The emergency shuttle lands and two more of our healers scramble out with a hoverboard. After conferring briefly with Jax, they carefully move her upon it. I back away, sensing that my part in her rescue is done. The sickly queen's hand darts out, hard and fast around my wrist, setting off my camouflage again. She rasps, "Find Lish. She won't make it on her own."

Placing my other hand over hers, I vow to do just that. "Rest easy, Queen Trovena. We will not stop looking until she is recovered and safely at your side once more."

It takes her a moment to let go and I think she wants to say something more but the words do not come. I'm too choked up to speak when I turn to the others. They're all staring at me, clearly in awe of my tracking abilities. Straightening my spine, I tuck my wings neatly behind me and step forward ready to continue the hunt.

I SQUAT DOWN ON THE ROOF WE STAYED ON THE NIGHT I first escaped. It's the place where Lady and I first started our friendship. Worry twists in my gut as I watch the scene slowly unfolding before me. The huge dragon-like warrior is so careful with my friend that I think she might have a chance. I realized earlier today that something was wrong. Trying to keep my worry at bay, I kept feeding her hydration tablets all day to counteract the overheated environment of the tiny room. Unfortunately, she never seemed to recover from that last run when the first dragon guy confronted us. I'm not doing so well either. My thoughts are disorganized and my thinking is fuzzy, like I'm lightheaded.

Peering over the side of the roofline, I watch other dragon men arrive. They all fuss over Lady and appear to be rendering first aid. A shuttle lands and I think the men who get out are doctors. There's a strange design on their shuttle and they take her away on a hovering backboard. I pray they're taking her to a hospital of some sort. I'm not taking any chances, so I follow the shuttle as best I can when it takes off. It's heading for the large flat area of tarmac where all the alien ships land. Running as fast as I can in my weakened state I lose sight of the shuttle within minutes. Scurrying up a tree near the large tarmac gives me a bird's eye view of what's going on.

The shuttle has already touched down beside a much larger transport vessel. Yet more dragon men have come pouring out. I'm just in time to see them disappearing into the ship with her. She's covered with a thin spread that billows out around the edges, making me think it's a cooling blanket of some kind. It dawns on me that she's probably suffering from heat stroke. At least they appear to be taking good care of her.

Everything looks on the up and up but one can never tell what's going to happen once they have you in their ship. I know that better than most. My hands cling tightly to the thick rough tree branch holding my weight until my knuckles are white. Chewing my bottom lip I try to figure out how to get on board that ship so I can make sure she's not going to be held against her will. Once that ship takes off, I'll never see her again and that makes my stomach twist with anxiety. I can't stand the thought of Lady and her baby being enslaved like I was.

Blinking back the tears, I climb back down the tree and swing down as far as I can before dropping onto my feet. I begin moving closer to the tarmac, hoping to come up with some kind of plan along the way. A strangled cry breaks from my throat when I see one of the huge dragon warriors touching down on the ground in front of me. It's the purple one. His wings are moving gently in the breeze and he lands without a sound. I back up too fast, tripping over a tree branch. In my haste to get away, I lose my balance and my ass hits the ground. Another dragon man is behind me and his strong arms grasp at me. I can't tell if he's trying to help me up or grab me. I immediately shove away and make a run for the nearest sewer. If they catch me, I'll be a slave again. I can't let that happen. I won't be able to save Lady if I'm in chains.

The smaller one begins to chase me but his friend stops him. He must be the leader because the purple one is slightly larger and the second dragon guy listens to and obeys him. Before I get more than a few feet, the one who held Lady is in front of me. He doesn't look threatening but I'm terrified anyways because there are three of them and I don't know what they want from me. They slowly close ranks and I'm trapped between the three of them.

They appear to be talking to each other. The noises are strange chirps and rumblings that don't seem like language. I know it is because it can't be anything else. Worry eats at me that they're trying to figure out how to capture me without breaking me. The green one backs away and the purple one inches closer to me. I glance over at the one who helped Lady and he's changing colors in the moonlight. It get the feeling that he's as anxious as I am. The purple one digs into his pocket for a hydration pellet, only his is strange because it's filled with bright pink fluid. My throat is parched but I'm worried that he's trying to drug me.

He makes a gesture for me to put it in my mouth, making more sounds that seem almost like words. It sounds like the background noise in a dream that you can't quite make out. Instead of doing as he wants, I dodge around him and try to get away. Unfortunately, another dragon man touches down in front of me. When I turn, he's flapping wings so delicate they remind me of fairy wings. The only direction left to me is towards the tarmac. If I can manage to avoid getting snared by them, I might be able to hide among the ships.

Suddenly, the large purple dragon man holds up one hand. When they all freeze, he tucks his wings behind his back and moves slowly forward. When I jerk back, he stops. I watch him wrap the hydration pellet in a scrap of cloth. He ties the ends and then makes a motion to toss it to me. Since they're not going to let this go, I hold out my hands to catch it when it sails across the space between us.

This pellet is larger and weightier than the ones we normally get. It's the bright pink color that worries me, because I've never seen anything like it before. He bends down and slides a little metal gun across the ground to me. A tree root stops it not more than two feet in front of me. His eyes look up, finding mine. For a brief second, we connect. I can almost feel his heart beating wildly in his chest. It's a double thump that I hear in my head so plainly it scares me. His head tilts slightly, and when his wings drop, I think he feels it too. He presses a finger to the space behind his ear and grinds out, "Giiveeeworedsss."

In a flash, I know what he's trying to communicate. Picking the tiny gun up, I recognize it as the device that implants alien language chips. The design is universal and therefore easily recognizable. The Strovians were implementing us with the chips in us right before I was taken. The other women were raving about how the knowledge of dozens of different species popped up as needed. It was effortless, not very painful and never needed replacing.

I want to place it behind my ear and pull the trigger, but I can't bring myself to trust my good fortune. What if this is a trap? They've already got Lady and she's counting on me to make sure she gets released when she's well.

I make a split-second decision. Dropping both the hydration pellet and the translation device into the pocket of my robe, I turn and bolt for the tarmac. There is a flurry of excitement and then two of the men are hot on my heels, but I already know they'll never catch me. They've got wings and the ships are one gigantic maze that will provide lots of tight spaces and shadows to aid my escape. My slight form slips easily through a few tight spaces, while they struggle and growl their displeasure at having to look for alternate routes. I grin like a mad fool, proud that I gave them the slip.

The moment I find the cover of darkness, I unfasten my cloak and turn it inside out. The moment it closes around me, I dodge to the side, slip up and around the men pursuing me, and disappear into the bustling evening foot traffic of the city. At one point I see them circling overhead, but they're looking for a dark cloak, not a sandy brown one that lets me blend into the sandy ground. I make my way to the far side of the city and into the dry brush.

Settling down for the night, the gravity of the situation hits me like a ton of bricks. I'm totally and utterly alone on this alien world. Without Lady to speak for me, I'll never secure work on my own. The food she gets is seasonal and hard to find. I'm going to die here and not one single person in the 'verse will know, much less care. Except Lady, I remind myself. She's the only one who'll miss me.

My throat is parched and my stomach is churning. With shaking hands I take out the big hydration pellet the dragon men gave me. It looks lush and refreshing. Holding it up, I can almost see different shades of pink swirling around in the pellet. It's round, relatively flat and has a clear coating. I don't have much of a choice. I can starve, die of dehydration or chance taking this hydration pellet. I worry that it was designed to make me fall into a drug-induced slumber. My mouth waters at the sight of the liquid. I'm taking it because

I can't resist. At least there is no one around to abduct me if it knocks me out.

Before I can keep vacillating over my decision, I cram the oversized pellet into my mouth. The coating dissolves almost immediately and I feel a gush of liquid on my tongue. Swallowing it down, I notice it's thicker and more luxurious than any hydration I've ever had. It must have contained some medication because it coats my dry throat and I not only feel energized but my thirst is immediately quenched.

After a few moments of not feeling drowsy, I reach back into my pocket and pull out the tiny gun containing the translation chip. The black metal is cool as I turn it over in my hand.

*Giiveeeworedsss.* The alien dragon man's words whisper through my mind. How does he speak my language? Why are they so focused on getting their hands on me? My mind is no longer sluggish so the answer comes easily. They want to cash in on the reward.

Still, I want to be able to understand what every alien is saying more than anything in the universe right now. If I could communicate with the locals, I might be able to survive here. A thought pops into my head. I might be able to convince one of the locals we've worked for to help me get Lady back off the dragon ship and make sure they don't take her young.

My hand moves the gun to my neck before I've really decided that's what I want to do. I press the tiny barrel right against the bony cartridge behind my ear and press the trigger before I chicken out. There's a prick and then a thump. My mind's going a mile a minute. I think the prick was the introduction of something to dull the pain of the deeper penetration of the chip being shot into my neck.

My eyes water and my trembling hand releases the gun. It clatters when it hits the ground. After that everything is eerily silent. It seems like a sad metaphor for my life. I'm sick and tired of being alone and miss the one and only friend I've had in years. Granted we didn't spend a lot of time talking and I know next to nothing about her, but Lady was another lost soul like me. Her strange alien face rises in my mind and I can't help the tears that slide down my face.

I bitterly miss the nice new life that was stolen from me when I was abducted years ago. If I'd arrived safely at my destination, there would have been a handsome alien husband and a better life waiting for me. It all seems like such a distant and impossible dream. No man would have me after I've been enslaved, and then homeless and eating out of the trash for months on whatever the hell alien planet this is.

I know that tomorrow's another day and I have to wake up, pull myself up by my nonexistent bootstraps and get on with living. However, for just tonight I'm going to feel sorry for myself, grieve my losses and fall asleep with tears running down my stupid face. Every single time I think this is my darkest hour, things just get worse and I'm sick and tired of it.

HATCH LOWERS THE BINOCULARS AND SWIVELS AROUND to look at me. His expression is both pleased and a little smug. "It appears that you were correct. Giving her some time to herself was the way to get her to hydrate and accept the translation chip we gifted her with."

I glance out into the distance, barely able to make out her resting form. "Queens are stubborn and willful creatures, commander. Even the most docile human will not accept commands given by a male."

"Allowing her time to calm down was beneficial. Having a breeder in our clade is helpful."

Shock rolls through me. "I'm not of your clade. I have a father and siblings. They are my clade."

Hatch turns to face me. His expression is serious. "Do you intend to seek out a queen to mate with your father at your side?"

I jerk back, horrified at the prospect of such a thing. "Of course not!"

"Then you wish a queen for all your own."

My wings droop. "I'm yet young to be thinking of taking

a mate." Glancing back at the now slumbering queen, I now know a fierce want deep in my soul. It is a burning need that was not there before. "This queen affects me."

"As she does me and the rest of my clade." He gives me a knowing look and I realize he is referring to Jax and possibly Drac. "We are three. Adding a true breeder would better position our clade to serve a queen."

"I see the wisdom in your words. Where we might falter on our own, a clade would ensure our queen is always protected while we go about our duties on our new home world." I can't stop myself from looking at her yet again. My tongue comes out to slide against my lower lip. "I just never thought to have a queen when first starting out in life."

"Why wait to enjoy the touch of a human queen when we can share this one?"

"You assume much if you think she will accept us. Human queens prefer to breed one queen to one male. No matter if he be a breeder or warrior, they like the one-on-one bond. You well know this, Hatch."

"I believe most males think they can manage a queen on their own, and once they are chosen all other activities fall away, leaving only their dedication to their queen. I am not so willing to forgo the ways of a warrior even for breeding rights to a lovely human queen. Some have been known to accept a tri-bond. What's one more on top of that, especially if we trade off time at her side?"

"You tempt me with the one luxury that's difficult for any male to decline." It's taken this male I barely know moments to get me interested in joining his clade. "I will make no hasty decision about joining your clade. Let us tend to the needs of this mysterious queen. If she warms to us, then let us talk more about how to best serve her needs."

His hand lands on my shoulder and his serious expression turns pleased again. "I respect you more for not jumping recklessly into a situation without giving it proper consideration."

My body relaxes and only then do I realize how tense this exchange has been. Peering back into his binoculars, he sighs. "You may take the first watch over our new queen, if it pleases you."

My need for her doubles in an instant. "I do wish it."

Taking the binoculars from his face, he hands them to me. "You do not wish to take your eyes off her, am I correct?"

Taking the binoculars from him, I raise them to my eyes and focus on her beautiful face. She's slight, pale, and her features are delicate. "She reminds me of the fragile flowers that grow in our new hydroponics unit. I cannot imagine moving through the 'verse with no plating to protect my skin or wings to carry me rapidly from danger."

Hatch's voice turns almost hoarse. "This lost queen needs to be covered by kind and benevolent warriors more than any I have seen. It is my understanding that the more hardship they've endured, the less they like to be left alone."

That seals her fate with me. "She needs us almost as much as we need her."

"Perhaps more, my friend. Do not take your eyes off her this night, for she may well be our future queen, if the gods are willing."

I stand taller, knowing Hatch trusts me to protect our new queen. A little voice in the back of my head disapproves of me using that term since she's not chosen us. "We must make proper provisions for her care."

"My clade has been preparing for almost a full solar revolution. I have tasked Jax with retrieving our provisions.

Drac will relieve you and we will make a nest fit for such a lovely queen."

"It will be as you say for now, commander."

I feel him move away and find that I am happier than I've ever been. To have a queen to protect is the one fantasy it never occurred to me to dream. There are so few queens and so many warriors, it seemed farfetched to hope to be chosen from among so many.

As the hours pass, I grow ever more excited. According to the Sonarian, Lish is her name. It's a strange name for such a beautiful creature. She administered the translation chip with shaking hands.

I know Hatch is negotiating with the peacekeeper to have her remanded to our care. It occurs to me that my father might be willing to plead our case with Queen Daisy. If another human vouched for us in this situation it might make a difference.

I ease out my communications device and thumb in his designation. His chipper voice answers instantly. "Greetings. How goes the parts acquisition, my son?"

"Greetings, father. Our team has sourced few parts and I have found none."

"You are not distinguishing yourself this day." His voice is disappointed. "You must try harder and remain on task."

"That mission is on hold."

"I was not told your orders have changed."

I quickly explain before his anger escalates. "I found a human queen. She is being hunted by a local peacekeeper who intends to return her to Earth. She is not doing well but refuses to allow us to assist her."

"You are certain she is in need of protection?"

"From many individuals, not least of which is my commander who seeks to entice her to join his clade. The peacekeeper is intent on returning her safely to her people."

"Did you tell your commander that now is no time for courtship? Her safety must come before all else."

"I am covering her, even now. She is in no danger from others." I pause, trying to figure out a nice way to explain my personal situation. "My commander wishes me to join his clade, no doubt thinking a breeder would go a long way towards garnering her interest in joining his clade."

"You are barely of an age to breed." His voice has suddenly turned cautious. "Do you wish to present yourself for her inspection?"

Taking a deep breath, I speak the words clawing to get out of my throat. "I do wish to be chosen by Queen Lish. The more I watch over her the more I want her. Though one such as me would have a difficult time covering a queen all on my own, my brethren seem like good males and together we could care for her properly. Several of the human queens have accepted clades rather than attention from individual warriors. It makes sense to me that we can provide better for her needs together than any of us can hope to manage individually."

"Did you contact me in hopes of gaining my approval for the group pairing?"

"Not exactly. Such pairings are the way among our people. Therefore, it never occurred to me that you wouldn't approve."

"Agreed. What do you wish of me?"

"I wish you to advocate our cause to Queen Daisy. Perhaps she can talk to the peacekeeper on our behalf. If he quits his claim to her, there is a chance we can convince her to visit our ship. Once she talks with the other queens, she will feel safe among us."

"It is a good and clever plan. Just know that your new clade may do everything right and this queen still might only choose one or none of you."

"Of course we understand this, my sire."

"Very well, I will speak with Queen Daisy. She will be worried to think a sister queen is stranded on an alien world with no protector."

Something loosens in my chest. "Thank you, my sire. I am grateful for your assistance in this matter."

"Helping my scion find his way to a good mate is one of my primary duties as your sire. It pleases me to render whatever assistance I can in this situation."

"My queen awakes. I must go, father."

"I will contact you when I have news, good or bad."

The stream ends and I tuck the com device back onto my belt. Staring through the binoculars, I see my new queen moving about in her sleep. Her arms are flailing and she's kicking her feet against the ground. Her behavior alarms me because it looks like she is being attacked in her dream world. Unable to bear seeing her so distraught, I approach stealthily.

Kneeling beside her, I place one hand on her shoulder. Her arms come out to push me away before her eyes open. A scream rends the air and she is suddenly awake and scrambling back from my touch. It makes me feel repulsive, though I know that I am not.

"Quiet, my queen. You were having a bad dream."

Her eyes squint like she thinks I might still be a specter from her dream. I hold my hands out so she can see I mean her no harm. "My name is Kane. I mean you no harm."

She blinks, looking confused. "I can understand you."

She sounds frightened and I think it might be my deep

voice, so rather than answer her, I tap behind my right ear to remind her that she administered the translation chip.

She rubs the same spot behind her own ear. "This is really weird. Can I understand everyone?"

Nodding, I murmur, "Yes."

Looking around suspiciously, she rubs her hands up and down her arms. It's a gesture that communicates she is cold. Before I can attend to that need, she asks about Drac. "Who was the man who helped my friend, the one who changed colors?"

"His name is Drac. He looked after her until our healers arrived."

She backs up a little further. "How is she?"

Bringing my hand to the com device resting on my hip, I gesture to it. "Our healers report Queen Trovena and her young are well. She is worried for you. She asked Drac to find you."

"She did? I want to see her."

Trying to remain calm, I explain. "Your friend has been taken to our vessel. She was very ill and needs time to recover."

"I want to speak to the male, Drac. Is that possible?"

"I can call him to come speak with you."

I nod and thumb him a message on the com that our queen wishes to speak only to him. I won't risk our entire clade descending upon her when she's just calmed herself enough to dialogue with us. When I'm finished, I remain quiet, letting her take the lead. She looks everywhere but at me, paying attention mostly to the sky. My spirits lift when I realize she is on the lookout for the older warrior.

When he lands moments later, she slowly comes to her feet. Having her eyes on him rattles Drac. He forgets to

kneel until she is a few steps away and then drops respectfully to one knee. Better late than never, I think.

Turning her eyes to me, she asks cautiously, "Can you
leave us alone? I want to have a word with him."

I jump to my feet and begin backing away. I see the tips
of Drac's wings tremble slightly. It's a stark reminder that
on an instinctual level warriors are still terrified of queens.
Only instead of worrying that they'll reap us, like the
Draconian queens of old, we now worry incessantly about
displeasing or unintentionally frightening them. I make
haste to follow Queen Lish's orders, lest I break the fragile
trust we are slowly building.

## 8 / BUILDING TRUST
### LATISHA

I DON'T KNOW WHY THESE MEN ARE DOING WHAT I SAY. It's a bit unnerving but a pleasant surprise compared to what I'm used to. Normally aliens just run right over me or snub me like a lesser being. This is the one that Lady asked to look for me, so he's the only one I even come close to trusting. Granted I don't really trust him, but these aliens seem different from the others I've met.

Standing here, staring down at this one, I can't figure out why he's kneeling. He's big and strong and kind of scarred. I want to talk to him but the words won't come. My knees are shaking and I don't think I can take a step without collapsing onto the ground. I need to pull my mess together and figure out what happened to my friend.

I remember how he lifted her and held her in his arms. How gentle and respectful he was with her. I was there on the building, watching it all. He looked worried sick about her and it hit home with me because I was feeling the same way. She must have asked him to find me for a reason. My gut tells me that she needs me. Can I trust him to take me to her?

Finally he speaks, probably because he thinks I'm not going to. "What do you wish of me, my queen?"

That wasn't what I expected him to say. I skip right over the possessive term and the fact that he called me a queen. That probably just means woman. I can see how the translator might make that mistake.

"I want information on my friend, the one your people call Trovena. The one who called himself Kane said she went to your ship."

Without looking up, he responds quietly, "She is in our healing unit. Do you wish to speak to her? I can raise her on my com unit."

My mouth drops open because literally nothing in my life is ever this easy.

I mimic his formal speech. "I wish it."

Before I can blink, he pulls something from his waist and begins pushing buttons. Funny, I would have thought advanced beings would voice prompt all their devices. I guess not. He eventually mumbles into the device but I'm not quite close enough to catch what he says.

Suddenly, Lady's voice sounds loud and clear. "Did you find my friend, Warrior Drac?"

"Yes, Queen Trovena. She wishes to speak with you."

Suddenly, my feet are moving towards the large warrior. "Trovena, I'm here. Are you well?" Using her real name for the first time is surreal.

"No, I am much weakened by our recent time of deprivation. I am pleased the Draconian warriors have seen fit to load my language into your brain."

"Yeah, that was all kinds of weird but I can understand every single word now."

"I wish you to come aboard their ship and meet with me. We have much to discuss, you and I."

Her cryptic words send my mind spiraling out of control with worry. "Are you safe? Now that I can understand languages, I can advocate on your behalf."

Only we both know I can't because I'll be taken prisoner again. I bite my lip and wait for her to think over my offer. A short silence spins out between us while the dragon warrior just sits there, on two knees instead of one now.

Finally, she speaks. "Come to me. We are safe for now."

"Okay, I'll come as soon as I can."

"I await your arrival." Her voice sounds exhausted all of a sudden and it ratchets up my anxiety. I see her lower her head back to the sleeping platform and her eyes drift closed as the com goes blank.

It takes everything I've got to make my next move. "Will you take me to the healing center aboard your ship?"

"My clade will escort you safely to your friend queen. We will make arrangements for you to see her the moment she is awake and accepting visitors again."

I'm right about the word queen meaning woman. Perhaps the translation program is substituting clan for clade. I immediately shake my head. "No. I don't want the others around me." An image flits through my mind. They're hauling me through the air, tossing me from man to man as they fly around, laughing at my horrified screams. I know that's just my primitive fears coming out to play, but I can't shake the panic I feel at the thought of being surrounded by them. "I only trust you. You helped my friend. You were nice and gentle with her. I want you to escort me."

At some point his head has come up and he's staring at me with intense dark eyes. I swallow down my fear and step closer to him. He's not going to eat me, I tell myself. Then I feel stupid for thinking he would.

"It will be as you wish, my queen." He's calling me his again. I suspect he doesn't mean anything by it but it conjures all kinds of thoughts. Thoughts of me being locked in his personal space, of him grabbing me and of him on top of me doing things I haven't thought about in forever. Instead of panic, a wash of pure heat practically consumes me.

His nostrils flare and his wings lift up slightly. Something got his attention. I can't imagine what it is, but he comes to his feet. Closing the distance between us, he keeps his hands clasped in front of him as if to prove he's a gentleman. One wing comes out and slips around me. Before I know what's happening, he's drawing me to him.

"I will shelter you under my wing. No harm will come to you as long as I am your protector."

I exhale a breath, trying to get my own arousal under control. Nothing about this situation is safe, much less sexy. I feel like crap for thinking about him this way when he's only trying to rescue me. I've been through an ordeal these last few years, so maybe it's natural to fancy the first man who treats me with a modicum of respect. His voice is soothing and kind. What he says about protecting me sounds all kinds of good. I'll be safe for the duration of our trip to the ship but then I'll be on my own again. Moments after being folded to his side, I realize his body heat and wing are warming me. I hadn't realized my teeth were chattering until they stopped. This feeling of being sheltered and protected is such a relief after everything I've been through that it's making me tear up.

A hand comes around behind me and gently pats my arm. "Do not worry, little queen. Your friend is recovering. She has commanded us to find you and bring you to her side. We will not fail in that mission."

The worry twisting in my gut doubles. It sounds like we may have to pass through a war zone to get to his shuttle. I shove down my anxiety and try to focus on the here and now. Since I'm the most socially awkward person on this alien world, I choke out, "Drac's a nice name. Does it mean something special?"

His feet freeze for the briefest of seconds then we're moving again. "It means dragon. My queen mother took one look at me and did not see anything special enough to warrant a name. There are many with my name among the warrior class."

That's such a horrible story that it makes my chest hurt. "I wish we could rename you hero. You did rescue my friend after all, and now you're rescuing me as well."

Suddenly, he's looking down at me. Although he's not actually smiling, his face is beaming with happiness. He likes being complimented. Maybe he's not dangerous after all.

"If it pleases my queen to call me such, I will answer to it."

Sweet day in the morning, this strange dragon man just let me change his name. Without really thinking about it, my hand comes out and covers the larger one still resting on my arm. This man's an odd mixture of terrifying and naive. He seems almost innocent about women. It's sweet and allows me to lower my guard just a little. My anxiety dips down to something realistically manageable for the first time in forever. It's such a relief that my hand grips him tighter.

His head snaps down to look at our joined hands. His brow creases. "Would you like me to fly you to our shuttle?"

I honestly can't even process what he just asked. He slowly bends to cradle me in his arms, lifting me against his chest. After jostling me into a more comfortable position he runs several steps, jumping into the air. Instead of landing back on our feet, we soar higher and higher until we're moving above the city. His gigantic wings are flapping enough to create a swirl of cool air around us.

So much for my anxiety being manageable. A strange dragon man is flying through the air with me in his arms. There are no safety belts or anything, just his strong arms holding me in place. I wrap my arms around his neck and hold on for dear life.

When my nose hits his chest, I discover it's solid muscle. He smells like almonds and licorice. I decide it's an enticing scent. It hits me that I'm choosing to focus on something insignificant to keep from freaking out. This isn't the first time my brain has pulled that little switcheroo. I just hold on and let my mind wander.

The wind blows through my hair and I'm angry with myself. Angry because I can't make myself be interested in this new flying experience. I should be looking at all the sights—people and buildings probably look tiny from this far up. At this altitude I could probably see majestic vistas. This is the one and only time I'm ever going to fly and I'm so terrified I'm hiding my face in this man's chest. I suck.

He shifts slightly and I find my nose pressing into his neck. His scent is changing. My hero's gone from smelling enticing to downright delicious. Without meaning to, I find myself nuzzling his neck just a tiny bit. It's wrong and taking advantage but I can't force myself to stop. A deep growl escapes from the back of his throat. He shifts again and tucks my head under his chin in midflight. Now I really feel awful for overstepping my boundaries with him. He's been nice to me and I've gone and made him mad. I vaguely realize that the stress of my situation has gotten the better of me and I just need to stop.

When we land on the tarmac, he growls at the other dragon men. Unlike the sound he made for me, this growl is dark and threatening. The others back up, covering their noses. I realize it's because I stink to the high heavens after not having a proper bath for I don't know how long. It's embarrassing but I didn't have a choice. I wrap my arms tighter around my protector's neck.

He strolls onto the shuttle with me and shuts the door with a voice prompt. After sitting me delicately on a chair and strapping me in, he expertly lifts the shuttle from the ground and plots a course to their ship. We appear to be the only two people on the shuttle so I force myself to relax. It's clear that he's got this.

The next thing I know, I jerk awake to find that he's carrying me through the ship. We stop in a strange room with a million lights interspersed with tiny fans that light up in a wave pattern and the fans on either side of each row buzz to life. My skin prickles. When I start to struggle, Hero murmurs something in a soothing tone and repositions me in his arms. I realize he said something about decontamination protocols. Looking down at my hand, I see the dirt and grime slowly disappear. My sleeve looks threadbare but clean by the end of the cycle, so I assume it's true with the rest of my body. It feels good to be clean at long last.

For some reason I can't force my eyes to stay open. I selfishly snuggle down into the big warrior's arms and just enjoy the warmth of his body and the scent of his skin. He tucks my head under his chin and leaves the moment the last of the lights go out and the door slides open. I guess I'm all decontaminated.

He eventually walks into a spacious suite and takes me

into a room with a huge bed. It's not really a bed but I can tell it's meant to represent one. Though it's floating, they've dressed it up like a human bed. I've never seen any other alien do that, so it makes me think there might be a human living here. My head's spinning too much to try to unravel that right now. I'm just too exhausted to keep my eyes open. He lays me on the platform and it's so soft and warm that I fall asleep again as he covers me with a thick soft blanket. My last thoughts are that I was supposed to be taken to Lady. Maybe I'm too late and she's sleeping right now too. I don't think of myself as a quitter but tonight I simply can't stay awake.

STANDING OVER MY NEW QUEEN, I FUSS WITH HER blankets and cushions. My large hands, gnarled with scars and imperfections, ensure her entire body is covered before I step back. This young queen is the most beautiful sight my eyes have ever landed on. She outshines all the others of her kind, for none have ever captured my notice before this day. This old warrior's wings droop like a youngling when I look upon her beauty.

My clade has been preparing for a queen for several lunars and now it appears we have secured the most perfect one out of them all. I can't take my eyes off her clean, pretty face and long strands of delicate hair. Her features are fine and totally feminine.

My queen has selected a new name for her protector. Rather than the generic name I've been called all my life, I now have one specifically chosen for me. I am now called Hero. Pride surges in my chest that although my own queen mother saw nothing special in me, this sweet human queen sees my value. Hero is the name I will be called moving forward, a name I will wear humbly.

I remember how soft her body was against mine when we flew. She was frightened and took comfort from me. I never would have thought to be the first she claimed, yet she did just that. She will make a good mate. She's kind, caring and gave me a name of worth. When she nuzzled her face against my skin I released my mating scent. This is something a warrior should never do without leave from his queen but my control slipped slightly.

My chest is filled with visions of her moving around our space. She's smiling and happy in my imaginary world of what could be. Every member of our clade will worship the ground she walks upon, if we decide to allow her feet to touch the ground again. We might just carry her everywhere since she's ours to protect.

The grim reality hits me that she really only accepted me as her protector and I'm not nearly enough for such a unique and elegant queen. Stepping back once more, I take up a position against the wall. Somehow I know, even though I am her Hero, she would not wish me in her personal space.

Standing guard over my own queen is a kind of pride I've never known. Just when I am beginning to think I can do this she begins to toss and turn in her sleep. Startled, I move near, careful not to wake her. As I edge closer, I can see her face is contorted in fear. She's mumbling something about being poked. Fury lights in my gut that someone would abuse her so.

She's clearly having a nightmare, reliving some horror or abuse from her past. I cannot allow her to suffer. Lowering myself onto the edge of the sleeping platform, my hands come out and gently wrap around her upper arms. I lightly shake her awake. She rouses with a start, her eyes wild with fear. After trying to scramble back out of my grip, she realizes I am her protector and sucks in a much needed breath of oxygen.

"You are aboard a Draconian vessel, safe in my keeping. No one can harm you anymore." Gazing into her slowly calming face, I wish the other members of my clan were here for they would have more reassuring words than me. Hatch has invited the breeder to join our clan. It is moments like this when he should be at her side. I am but a simple and rough warrior, yet I try my best to soothe the small human. "Are you well, my queen? Shall I gather other members of my clan to reassure you?"

"What? No, I was just having a bad dream."

"Do you wish to talk about it?"

Pressing her palms over her eyes, she is silent for so long that I begin to think she will not answer me. When her hands come down, she looks a bit lost. "Hero, I thought you were taking me to see Lady."

"The healers report she is sleeping. You fell asleep in my arms so I brought you to our quarters to rest."

"It's the middle of the night?"

"Draconian ships run off a forty-five-thousand micron cycle. One minute equals three microns. We work for three thousand microns and utilize the rest of the cycle for dining, rest and leisure."

"I see." The way she glances nervously around the room makes me think she might be anxious in a new environment or being alone with a lone scarred warrior. "I can locate a breeder if you would like a male with more experience caring for a queen."

Shaking her head slightly, she pulls her knees up and turns to look at me. "I don't want to meet any more new people. Lady told me to go with you, so she must trust you. Until she wakes up, I can stay alone."

Coming to my feet, I force myself to respond politely. "You wish me to leave?"

Staring up at me with huge eyes, my queen looks vulnerable chewing her bottom lip. "Where do you normally sleep?"

"My clan has quarters nearby. This room was created to house our queen."

Her mouth falls open. "I'm sleeping in some other woman's bed?"

When she begins to move, I throw up a hand. "No. This room was created to house a queen, should we be fortunate enough to secure one. It is normally standing empty."

As she relaxes back against the fluffy squares, I realize all our research on human queens is paying off. They luxuriate on the squares, so we did well by adding them to our stock. She nods. "I appreciate having a place to rest my head. Do you mind if I ask why you are still here?"

Swallowing thickly, I answer honestly. "It is my duty to stand guard over you."

The moment her lovely face falls into a frown, I quickly add, "I mean to say it is my honor to stand for you."

Scooting back away from me, she gestures to the large space before me. "There's plenty of space here for two. You stay all the way over there, though. No touching."

Kicking off my boots before she changes her mind I state firmly, "No Draconian male would ever touch a queen without being invited. The penalty is death."

Her stern expression slips away, replaced by one of amusement. "You touched me when you carried me."

Tugging apart the seal on my uniform, I gape at her softly spoken words. This queen is smiling so I do not think she is serious about having me punished. "Warriors touch queens to keep them safe. No other touch is permitted without approval."

Kicking off my uniform, I move towards the empty space wearing only my long undergarment. I freeze with one leg on the platform because the small queen is staring at me with her mouth hanging open. I move back and rush across the room, jerk a thin pullover top from one of the compartments that houses all our extra gear and pull it over my head. Wisely, I chose one with long sleeves, so the gentle creature will not be forced to look upon my many scars. This is apparently the correct choice because her mouth is now closed and she is pushing a fluffy square over to my side of the platform.

I can't help the grin that creases my face at the thought of reclining upon it like a queen. If my fellow warriors could see me now, they would have much to say about the situation. Still, I am among the luckiest of my kind for a queen has smiled upon me this day.

My queen wraps herself in the blanket, leaving none for me. I care not because I am almost overly warm wearing the clothing that I am. By and large warriors prefer to wear as little as possible to bed. Apparently queens are the opposite, because my queen is still wearing all her clothing. Taking a deep breath, I lay back and stare at the ceiling. Though I know that being quiet is expected, my head is filled with many thoughts of what might one day be. Perhaps our queen will accept us as her clan. If the breeder joins our clan, she might mate with him. If that happens, the room will be thick enough with pheromones to trigger parthenogenesis and then we can all spawn young. Never knowing a queen's touch is expected, but to be in the same room when a queen breeds would be a genuine honor.

Turning to look at her, I see her back is turned to me. I

wish to see her pretty face steeped in pleasure and her body taking one of my clan. My breath hitches when images of her choosing to breed with me pop into my head. Some human females chose plain warriors. If I am worthy, she might choose me at some point far in the future. That is a dream worth holding on to.

## Latisha

I can feel Hero shifting slightly on the bed but I squeeze my eyes shut and force myself to be still. If I don't look at him, I can pretend that I didn't just do what I did. My head is spinning with worries and thoughts I dare not admit, even to myself.

I invited a total stranger to sleep in the same bed with me. Allowing that to sink in for a moment, I'm in awe of myself. Why did I do that?

Clearly it was because he makes me feel safe. Lady signaled that I could trust him and he's been nothing but respectful. I need to feel safe right now. I haven't felt that in a long time. Maybe nothing bad would happen if he left me alone in his clan quarters. My head fills with huge not-nice warriors breaking into the room and hauling me off to poke, prod and laugh at. The huge dragon warriors are so much larger and stronger than me that they could force me to do a million things I don't want. That's why I asked him to stay, for safety.

A little voice in the back of my mind whispers, "Liar," and it's true. I might want him for protection but I also have eyes to see, so I can't help but notice he's really sexy. Some aliens I've met were attractive and others are kind of repulsive. Though I'd never have sex with a total stranger, I'm forced to admit this hunk of a man makes my core dampen.

He's larger than most males I've seen but that doesn't bother me at all.

The reality of my situation slams through my brain. I'm attracted to a huge alien with scales, claws and gigantic wings. How does he get comfortable lying on those wings to sleep? Maybe that's why he's shifting around. He has broad shoulders and markings on his skin that look like some vestigial form of scales. I remind myself that the scales don't look real. They're just faint markings, an echo of the scales worn by his ancient ancestors.

His skin changes colors to match my own when we touch. Even now, because I am in close proximity, his tone is a light creamy ivory with a hint of pink. Something about his entire body morphing because I'm near kicks up my desire for him. It's like he was made just for me. That's crazy talk, but I feel it all the way down to my core.

An image rises in my mind of his backside as his uniform came off. Shock rolls through my gut all over again at the size of his tail. No, I'm shocked that he has one in the first place. It's thick near his lower back and tapers down to a gently rounded tip around his ankles. He keeps it lifted slightly so it doesn't drag on the ground. I wonder if he uses it to hit his enemies in battle or if the tip is used to pleasure his female. Way to go, Latisha. I can't believe my mind went there.

His mother named him the Draconian equivalent of boy or human. What mother would do that to her own child? Anger fires in my chest at the thought that he's lived his whole life with that kind of humiliation hanging over his head. Every time someone said his name it would have been a reminder that he was nothing special. Correcting that injustice had been a genuine pleasure. Was it arrogant and pompous to rename a person you just met? It normally would be considered extremely inappropriate, but the big dragon warrior's expression practically melted into something approaching adoring when I suggested he should have been named Hero. He deserved better than a generic descriptor for a namesake and now he has one that's special and uniquely for him. I don't feel bad about it.

There's no escaping the fact that he's fascinating on a lot of levels. It would be disingenuous to tell myself that I want to keep him at my side for protection only. It's important for a woman to be honest, at least with herself. His erotic body and gentle handling of me is drawing me to him. I want him right there beside me, not off in some other part of the ship pleasuring a choice female with that sexy tail of his. I want him right here, making me feel not only safe but valued as a person. I fall asleep luxuriating in his masculine scent.

JAX

WATCHING HATCH PACE BACK AND FORTH, I CONTINUE packing Drac's belongings. It's almost beyond belief that our oldest and most scarred warrior was chosen first by our new queen. I was the one who campaigned to add Drac to our clade and am proud that he's made such a positive impression upon Queen Latisha. If he gains her favor, it is more likely that she will accept us. Though both Drac and Hatch are convinced that she is our one, I will not commit until I know more of her personality. They may be satisfied with a beautiful female but I have no intention of spending all the years of my long life with a spoiled demanding female or one who plays us off against each other. Most human queens are lovely people, but it stands to reason there must be some among them that are not suitable for mating. I will know for sure before I give my seal of approval for this union.

Hatch stops short in front of me. When I look up, his expression evidences his frustration. "I think we should turn on the security feed."

Dropping Drac's last uniform into the huge trunk, I

straighten. Though I am smaller in stature and younger, I stand my ground. "That is a poor idea. Human females prefer to mate in private. She will think less of us for spying upon her during an intimacy with her chosen male."

"Perhaps they are not being intimate."

"It matters not. If they are, we should not be watching without her permission. If they are not sharing sex, then he is standing guard because she's afraid. It will only make her more wary of us if she discovers we spied upon her while she slept."

Running a hand over his head, Hatch turns and begins pacing again. "Of all of us to choose from, why did she select Drac? He's not a breeder, nor is he human sized. He knows nothing of human queens."

"You know the humans love unique warriors. Though we see Drac as plain, his size, markings and camouflaging abilities might make him more distinctive in her eyes. He's also polite and respectful. Even with no experience tending to a queen, he's smart enough to provide intelligent conversation."

"You did well by insisting upon having him in our clade. I thank you for being persistent."

Turning to face our clade leader, I ask curiously, "Has it once occurred to you that she might not be to our liking?"

His feet come to a stuttering stop, almost causing him to trip, and his tail spins around to stabilize his oversized body. The expression on his face would be comical if this situation didn't involve the most important decision of our entire life.

"Human queens are all beautiful and this one needs our protection."

"For all we know, she could have a bad disposition or

irritating personal habits." I give him a moment to let that sink in before continuing.

"What are you suggesting, Jax? I have no intention of allowing such a needy and beautiful queen to slip through our claws because you have anxieties about her disposition."

"Rather than luring any mate we can, I think we should consider our time with her an interview of sorts." When he opens his mouth to object, I quickly add, "Think about it for a moment. We have been trained to think that queens can do no wrong. We were taught this by Draconian queens who were horribly abusive to their males. Since humans seem to be the opposite in personality to our former masters we assume they are all kind and loving. They can't all be good, Hatch."

"I've never seen one who wasn't devoted to her male."

"In the before times we only knew what the Draconian queens taught us. Since escaping their grasp we have the luxury of thinking for ourselves. Will you risk our future happiness on the blind belief that queens can do no wrong? What of our young? We must choose a female who respects our right to breed and will treat them with kindness and affection."

The wisdom of my words finally hits home and his expression transforms into one of grudging acceptance. "I see you have given this queen some thought. Your argument has merit. We will spend time getting to know this beautiful queen and be certain we grow a liking for her before asking her to join our clade. I will make it clear she must accept all of us or none of us."

Breathing out a sigh of relief, I drop my hands to my sides. Gaining his support in this matter turned out to be much easier than I anticipated. I feel validated and heard by the leader of our clade. "Thank you, Hatch. I wish our lives together to be pleasant and agreeable for all. Has Kane decided if he wishes to join our clade?"

"He wishes to give our request the consideration such a weighty decision deserves."

"I doubt we would be able to lure another breeder if he turns us down."

"You are a healer, Jax. You know almost as much about queens as a breeder. Human females have a strong preference for certain disciplines. Since I am a commander and you are a healer, that positions us well to be accepted by the queen we are now courting. She has clearly accepted Drac. If we like her, it will not matter so much if we have a breeder among our clade."

"I know how to treat medical conditions. Kane knows how to soothe a queen when she is upset and how to please her sexually. He understands how they think and can anticipate their needs in ways I cannot."

Before Hatch can respond their com sounds. Hatch voice prompts the com channel to open and Drac's face shimmers into view. He's wearing a clean uniform and the blank expression warriors are taught to maintain. I can see our new queen moving around in the background. Irritatingly enough, she seems to be straightening the room and making the bed. Gods of chaos, cleaning is something males do for their queens, not vice versa.

Hatch asked cautiously, "Is all well with Queen Latisha, Drac?"

Bowing his head slightly, his expression shifts to one of happiness when he lifts his eyes. "I was chosen as her protector and invited to sleep beside our queen last night. Our queen has also seen fit to bestow a new name upon me. I am now called Hero."

Hatch is genuinely pleased with this turn of events. His

feelings are evidenced in his warm reply. "Your new name suits you, my friend. Congratulations on being selected. You are well worthy of a queen's affection."

"Thank you, sir. Our queen now wishes to see her friend queen."

Jerking to attention, Hatch catches Hero's unspoken wish for us to come and spend time with her. "We will come right away to provide an escort."

"If it pleases you, perhaps Kane can come as well."

I speak up before Hatch can misstep. "We'll contact him and request that he come at once."

Hatch's head swivels around to look at me but he doesn't speak.

"We will await your arrival. Our queen is anxious to see Queen Trovena."

"We'll be quick about it."

When the screen goes dark, I quickly explain. "Drac, I mean Hero must suspect our queen might need the emotional support of a breeder. Her friend queen is well but not all of her young survived the birthing process. I do not know how Queen Latisha will react to that information since she spent so much time looking out for her pregnant queen friend."

Almost before I am done speaking Hatch brings his handheld com to his mouth and requests Kane come to our clade quarters at once. We head out to meet him as Hatch continues to explain our situation to Kane.

We stand in the main corridor until he arrives. He's out of breath and looks like he hasn't slept. "How goes the negotiation with the Arobian peacekeeper?"

Hatch shakes his head and his wings droop for an instant. "The stubborn male refuses to relinquish custody to us. He insists upon returning her to her home world. We must go to Earth and petition her to join our clade."

A frustrated growl escapes Kane's lips. "I do not like this Arobian forcing his will upon her. We should ask Queen Latisha and allow her to decide if she wishes to return to her home world."

I speak up quietly. "If she had wished to be on her own home world, she would not have signed up to be a galactic bride in the first place."

There are only grunts of agreement from the other two males. When we enter our clan quarters, I'm shocked to see them sitting side by side with Hero's wing wrapped snugly around her slight form. She is wearing one of the uniforms we set aside for our queen's use and I remember selecting this one myself. It is a deep blue, edged in silver. Hero's camouflage has shifted, making him mostly the same creamy pink as our new queen. His camouflage is malfunctioning a bit, as it blends in with the color of her uniform along the seam where their bodies meet. They look intimate because they are holding hands. Her head whips around to look at us and I wonder why she is so surprised to see us walk in.

Kane immediately apologizes. "Forgive the intrusion, my queen. We have come to escort you to the medical unit to see your friend queen."

Her head turns slowly around and she looks up at Hero. "Walking across this ship takes an escort of four males?"

Hero shoots Kane a quick glance before answering her question. "Our ship is safe. I simply wish us to spend time with the rest of my clan as much as possible."

I notice he uses the human term for clade. My translator makes no distinction between the two terms. Our glorious queen accepts his words without question and they both come to their feet. She makes no move to step away from him. It feels as though she enjoys being under his wing. Our Hero makes no attempt to introduce her to us by name. I think it is a good call not to overwhelm her with details at the moment. Once she sees her friend queen is well, she will be more amenable to thinking about us.

As we stand staring at her, a thousand thoughts fill my head. Surely Kane and Hatch are wondering the same things I am. Will she enjoy being under my wing? Will she snuggle herself close to me, as she does her new hero? Will she look to me for answers as she does him? Is her body as soft as it looks? Forcing my brain to stop generating questions that make my cock hard, I tighten my wings into a tight knot behind me.

Hatch motions Kane forward to walk on the other side of our new queen. Hatch is a clever male, always thinking long term. He relinquishes his place at her side in favor of Kane for a reason. It is done in hopes that being in close proximity to the lovely queen will result in Kane agreeing to join our clade. I will be surprised if he refuses. If so, it will only be because she rejects us all in favor of taking Hero in a one-on-one bond.

We head to the medical bay with Hero and Kane locking wings behind our queen. Hatch is in the lead and I walk behind, allowing my mind to ask more interesting questions about our queen. Is it possible for a queen to be as submissive as this one seems? She was defiant and avoidant when we were tracking her on the planet. One night in our clade quarters with Hero and she willingly allows us to lead her through the ship. I can't help but ask myself why she has had such a sudden change of heart. Perhaps I am a suspicious male and there is nothing sinister going on here.

Moving through the ship surrounded by Hero's clan is an experience I won't soon forget. I honestly feel like a queen with an official escort. Other males step out of our way. Their expressions are respectful but there is an undercurrent of something that looks like jealousy when they look at Hero and his clan. I immediately wonder if it's because they are with me and women are still rare among the Draconians. I have to admit when their eyes find me their expressions range from curious to admiring and a few display awed interest. I'm not all that attractive as far as human women go. On Earth I would be considered nothing special, but here I stand taller and carry myself with dignity because I feel more valued. It's a pleasant change from being treated like some kind of street urchin.

It's strange that Hero's clade all look so different. I would expect brothers and cousins to have more of a family resemblance but these four men are all very different in size, coloration and wing shape. A clan is extended family, right? Maybe they are distant cousins or something like that. I make a mental note to ask about that at some point.

Right now I'm eager to check on Lady. My feet stumble to a stop as I realize that I've done the same thing to my friend that Hero's mother did to him. I've given her a generic name. Forcing my feet to keep moving, shame fills my soul. When we were running around on the planet, all my time and energy was spent just trying to survive. One night in a real bed and a little food in my belly and now my brain is once again firing on all cylinders. That's apparently all it takes for me to see the stupid mistake I've made. It sickens me to the core.

The moment we enter the medical bay I spy my friend. She is on a large medical platform with several young around her. As we move closer, I count three little ones. They nuzzle closer to her now clean body. Without the layers of dirt we both carried during our time on Brackon Five I can see she is actually beautiful. Her emerald green fur is actually striped with solid black bands that run verti- cally up and over her body. Her tail is now fluffy and swishing back and forth as her young frolic. Her head lifts, and when her brilliant green eyes land on me, I can see her nostrils flaring. She smelled me before she saw me. That's interesting.

I rush to her bedside but before I can make my vocal cords form words, she speaks. "You came to me, Lish. I did not think you would."

Moving closer, I grin. "Of course I came. We've had each other's backs too long for me to even think of aban- doning you."

"You were frightened of the dragon warriors. Therefore, I doubted you would find the courage to allow them to escort you."

"You sent word for me to come with Hero, so I thought he must be trustworthy."

"His name is Drac. Does your translator mark the words as one and the same in your language?" Lady's smart. It only takes her a second to guess what's going on. "You renamed him." It's a statement, not a question. Her tone is slightly disapproving. That's how I know that I've made a social blunder.

Feeling ten kinds of conspicuous, I admit quietly, "Yeah, I guess I did."

Her majestic head turns to glance at Hero's clan before landing on me again. "We should talk alone." Her firm voice has me on alert. Something's definitely wrong and I clearly overlooked it.

I don't even need to ask the men to leave. They immediately melt back and reluctantly exit the room. Hero is the last one to slip through the door and gives me one long pensive look before turning to leave.

"Did I do something wrong? I watched how careful Hero was when he rescued you, and I decided to take a chance because you indicated the Draconians were to be trusted."

"First things first. You renamed a Draconian warrior." She doesn't seem angry necessarily, but her demeanor and tone of voice are deadly serious.

"About that, he explained how Drac's not really a name. Draconian mothers call Draconian children Drac if they're plain. He's really a nice person. Since he rescued us, I suggested a new name and he liked the idea."

Tilting her head in a gesture that's so human I almost smile, she ponders her next words as if choosing them carefully. "Are there actions humans take to lay claim to something they desire on Earth?"

For some reason children squabbling over treats immediately comes to mind. I grin as images of all the competitions I had with my siblings float through my mind. "When I was a kid, my siblings and I would race towards our tree-house and whoever touched it first got to be boss for the day." When she doesn't respond right away, I continue searching my brain for examples. "My brother always went that one step too far. I remember him licking every donut in the box because he knew none of us would want to eat one he'd slobbered all over. Also, we..."

"Stop. This is what you have done. Renaming the Draconian warrior is the equivalent of licking him on your world."

My mouth falls open and I just can't make myself understand what she's saying. My stunned brain lurches into gear once more and my stammering words come out defensive. "I... I didn't lick anyone. Hero agreed to be my protector, nothing more."

A wheezing sound comes from the back of her throat. It seems like frustration. "There are no females among the Draconians. Therefore, they seek alien mates. Humans are highly coveted among their people."

Still not getting it, I try to reason with her. "I asked for him because I saw how nice he was to you and I didn't know any of the other men. I trust what I see with my own eyes and hear with my own ears."

"Tell me about your trip to the ship."

Sighing, I go into a brief monologue about how he flew with me and I got sleepy so he took me to their clan quarters and we slept. I didn't agree to be anyone's mate so what she says makes less than no sense.

She pats the platform beside her and I gently sit down. I get the feeling that now that we can communicate, I'm about to get some kind of come to Jesus talk from her. Sure enough she explains the way of the world to me.

"What you describe is the way queens are claimed among the Draconians. You accepted him as your personal protector. To his mind, he now belongs to you. He sees you as his queen and therefore shelters you under his wing. Do you not see how special you are to him?"

Though I'm not special, my head fills with images of keeping Hero forever. He's big and strong. With him at my side, I'd never have to be afraid of anything. Something about that is appealing for a woman who's been bounced from one slave market to another for years. My face flushes when I think of staying cuddled under his wing and of having him in my bed. Maybe I could cuddle under his wing while we tumble off to sleep. I close down that train of thought just as my brain pulls up a mental image of his muscular backside with that thick tail.

My perceptive friend does not miss the gentle blush creeping up my face. "I see you are not opposed to having this clade for your own."

"Hero's really nice and respectful. I like him best of all the men I've ever met. I wouldn't mind getting to know him better."

Her face contorts into a mask of true disapproval. "You would separate him from his clade? I did not think you were a selfish female." She reaches out to draw her little ones closer. The snap in her voice makes me sit up and pay attention.

"I'm not sure I understand what you're annoyed with me about. I thought I was in trouble for leading Hero on. I'm trying to say that I'd like to explore the possibility of having a permanent relationship with him."

"Do you have any idea what an easy life I would have had on Brackon Five if I had allowed males to do favors for me in the hopes that I might want to mate with them?"

Anger fires in my gut. "Because I allowed him to share his quarters with me for one night, now I'm obligated to him. Is that what you're saying?" That shit's not going to fly with me, at all.

Sitting up abruptly, her voice drops. "You understand nothing of the 'verse. Shall I explain it to you as though you were a child?"

I wish she would break that shit down because I'm starting to get really riled up. Snapping my mouth shut, I give her a stiff nod. This woman has been good to me. I don't want to vent my anger about this situation on her because she's the one tasked with making me understand.

"Your Hero is a lone warrior. By his own admission, he is considered plain among his people. Therefore, he joined a clade to increase his probability of finding a mate. Draconians sometimes pool their resources, time and energy in order to ensure their female is afforded the best quality of life possible. You chose one warrior from a clade of four to be your protector. You gave him a name of honor. In doing so, you gave his life meaning and purpose. He will never leave your side unless you reject him. That kind of public humiliation would be a grave insult since you accepted his offer of protection already and spent time in his bed."

That makes sense. Rejecting the offer at the time it's made wouldn't sting because a woman wouldn't really know the man. Rejecting a man after getting to know him would hurt more, because you were rejecting them personally. The thought of hurting him stings more than it should for someone I've only known for a day. Wringing my hands in my lap, I speak up. "I'm not rejecting anyone at this point."

My friend relaxes back against the healing platform again. "Who do you think will be working long hours to provide the luxury you enjoyed last night when your warrior is forever at your side protecting you?"

Swallowing thickly, I realize how much I want that. The idea of having Hero with me all the time suddenly seems like the most important thing in my world. Fighting back the rising surge of possessive feelings for him, I protest weakly, "Well, I didn't know that protectors stayed with their mates that way."

"Your males joined a clade for a reason. If you truly wish to keep Hero, I suggest you investigate his reasons and consider accepting them all into your confidences."

"I can't have four husbands, I mean mates."

"Most females only wish for one mate. However, many in the 'verse choose two males, and taking three or even four is not unheard of among the Draconians."

"I believe love is between one female and one male."

"If your view of mating is that narrow, you should immediately reject the hospitality of Hero's clade. The longer you put it off the harder it will be for them to accept."

Guilt twists in my gut. I mumble to myself as I ponder the situation. "Four is simply too many. I'd never have enough time with each one. They'd end up being jealous of each other and they'd end up arguing over everything. It would be too much sex in general and too much negotiating between them for alone time. What if they want me to have sex with them all at the same time? I could never do something like that. It's just not physically possible." Try as I might, I just can't reconcile having four husbands with any happily ever after I've ever imagined.

"Those are all valid concerns about joining a clade. You should speak with your clade about such, Lish." Her voice now almost seems chipper.

My head jerks up to see her lifting one of her young to

lick its fur. I pick up one of them that's wandered over to paw and sniff at my clothing. "You sound like you think I should join their clan."

At this point, she's more focused on her little one than me. Murmuring between licks, she doesn't look up. "I believe you already did. Though that was clearly not your intention, you signaled acceptance of the one you licked at least." She pauses for a moment before speaking again. "Under threat of death, you are not to lick any of my young." She makes a little noise in the back of her throat that I've always thought of as laughter.

The mood around us shifts. "I didn't know you had such a robust sense of humor."

"It grieves me to know you were oblivious to my cutting wit over the last few lunars."

Ignoring her playful jab, I focus on her situation. "So, what's the plan for you and your little ones? They're adorable, by the way."

"We make for the Draconian home world. Queen Daisy has offered us sanctuary on the new Draconian home world. I accepted her generous offer, at least until my young are old enough to travel without fear of them developing a craving for space travel. That happens for some of my kind and they never wish to reside on a planet again."

Grinning, I can't help but be thrilled. "That means we're going to live on the same planet. I hope we're in close proximity so we can visit."

"I'm certain your clade has a shuttle. If this is so, they will be happy to transport you wherever you wish to go."

"Do women have jobs on the Draconian home world or do we all just make babies?"

Slapping one gigantic paw over a newborn wandering too far, she answers tartly, "I refuse to answer questions for you that you would be better served to ask your clade. You have nothing to fear from them for I have spoken with them all. Draconians follow the wishes of their females. If these males do not, simply scream for help and others of their kind will see that they are removed from your presence."

"That doesn't seem right. Wouldn't that make me the property of whichever warrior protects me?"

Shaking her head, she glances over my shoulder to the door. "You tire me with your endless questions. There are human queens aboard this vessel. Ask them questions until your head falls off or read through the Draconian database to get the information you seek. Sonarians do not enjoy prolonged conversation."

How could I have forgotten she was recently ill and just gave birth? Coming swiftly to my feet, I step back. "Sorry to pester you with my problems. I'm sure you need to rest and tend to your young. If you need any help with them, just let me know."

Her head snaps up and she pins me with a stern look before motioning to the door with one claw-tipped finger. "I can yet care for my own young, human. Go before I lose all patience for you this day."

I'm taken aback for a split second before I hear her making that laughing noise again. I've been had. It's shocking what an easy mark I'm turning out to be for my mischievous friend. I don't understand her humor but then again she's an alien so it's probably not reasonable to expect to get her jokes when we've only been able to communicate for such a short time.

The moment the door slides open, all four Draconians snap to attention. For some reason facing these four dragon warriors, knowing full well they want to make me their wife, is embarrassing. Still, I can't help but look at them with new eyes. They're a good-looking bunch of aliens. When they notice me giving them the once over, they stand straighter as if this is a form of inspection.

Hero steps closer, wrapping one wing around me. I don't object because if I'm being honest there is no place I'd rather be than under his enormous wing. His skin tone shifts to match mine almost immediately. Yep, he's been licked by me. There's no getting around that fact.

He speaks quietly. "I wish to introduce you to our clan."

He's using the term *our* which leads me to believe Trovena is right about him being under the impression he's been chosen. Then again, he's not wrong there, so I nod for him to continue. Gesturing is a weak form of communication but I'm overwhelmed and words are failing me at the moment.

The one with stripes on the edges of his uniform steps forward. Hero's voice is respectful but at the same time warm. "Hatch of the House Citron is the leader of our clade. He only recently achieved the rank of commander. Our mission to Brackon Five was the first in which he served in a leadership position."

Hatch steps forward but still keeps a good arm span away. "Greetings, Queen Lish. It is a pleasure to finally be able to speak with you."

"My name's actually Latisha. I guess Draconians would phrase it as Latisha of the House of Brogen." I dart a quick glance Hero and he nods in verification that their people would state my last name as a house name. To my mind that was kind of obvious but it's reassuring to know I'm right. "Trovena called me Lish because it was all she could make out of my language."

Hatch doesn't stumble at all in the conversation, making me feel like a bumbling fool by comparison. "Thank you for clarifying your namesake. I knew your name from the official bulletin but had assumed Lish was what humans refer to as a nickname."

Something about him having experience in human customs is reassuring. I don't have to be worried they'll take some minor misstep as a serious slight. "My family actually called me Tish when I was a child but I prefer Latisha." Clearing my throat, I try not to smile. "It sounds more grown up."

"You are fully grown and quite lovely to our eyes." Motioning over another of his clade, he intones, "Allow me to introduce Jax of the House of Citron. Jax is now a fully trained healer." Gesturing to Kane he continues, "This Kane of the House of Dreck."

Kane isn't a member of their clan. Since they don't explain anything about him, I don't ask. Maybe he's some kind of adjunct personnel on loan from another clan. I don't know anything about how their clans work. Something about the thought of him being an outsider makes me anxious. Pressing myself slightly closer to Hero, I wonder why Trovena wasn't aware that this clan only had three males. Brushing aside my worries, I extended my hand to the three new males in turn. "I'm pleased to meet you all." I know nothing of their work shifts or daily schedule so this might not be the time but I want answers. "Is there some place where we can speak privately? I have some questions that I believe only you can address."

Hatch steps back. "If you like we can take a formal meal in the dining hall. Our people use sound dampening devices to shroud our conversation from others. It is common, for on a ship there is often not enough space to find a secluded space when one wishes to discuss something private, nor is there always time to gather in one's quarters."

That makes sense. He's saying the only truly private space is their private quarters. Since everyone just got up and out for the day, no one's wild about going back there, especially since they haven't eaten yet.

They're all gazing at me. I suddenly realize how each of them is handsome in a different way. Hatch has a commanding presence. I see it now, where I didn't before. The man has an impressive set of black horns and intense dark eyes. They're all muscular except the medic. Jax is honestly the size of a human man. His stark green and black scales are offset by a pair of almost delicate wings. Where the others boast a huge wingspan, his would probably reach his fingertips if he stretched his arms out sideways. He's also the only one without a tail. It's like he comes from different stock altogether. Then there's Kane. Where the others are green, his scale pattern is purple. He's large but there's something about him that I can't quite put my finger on. The other two stand at attention as I look them over, but his stance is more relaxed and his expression almost flirtatious. All their expressions show a bit of heated interest, enough to make me blush.

I nod, choking out a one line reply to his offer of food and conversation. "I'd love to dine with you." I need to get over being tongue-tied around these men. It hits me that it's easier to speak my mind when I'm with only one of them.

The three of them draw together and whispers of a conversation drift to my ears. I raise one hand to toy with the seam on Hero's shirt. His hand covers mine and he tugs me closer. When he gazes down at me, there is such warmth in his dark eyes. His open acceptance is humbling. It makes me feel happy and wanted. We talked a little this morning and I feel totally comfortable with him. My eyes drop down to his lips. They're full and pale like his skin because he's mimicking my coloring. I can't help but wonder what kissing him would feel like. Just when I'm about to snatch a quick one, I hear wings fluttering around us.

I think the fluttering is a mannerism similar to clearing one's throat for a human. It's a gentle reminder that they are there and now ready to leave the area. I honestly appreciate their subtle non-verbal communication. It's also humbling to know these handsome devils are interested in making me their mate. I know that can't happen because I'm only one woman and they're four big strapping aliens, but part of me wishes it were possible.

Wʜᴇɴ ᴡᴇ ᴀʀᴇ sᴇᴛᴛʟᴇᴅ ᴀʀᴏᴜɴᴅ ᴀ ᴛᴀʙʟᴇ ɪɴ ᴛʜᴇ ᴍᴀɪɴ dining hall, we take turns filling plates as our lovely queen stares at the mixture of warriors and queens enjoying their own meals. I look around, pretending to see them for the first time in an attempt to ascertain what she's seeing and how she's interpreting their behavior.

While our queen chose utilitarian clothing, most of the other queens have chosen beautiful gowns. They also adorn themselves with jewelry, while Queen Latisha chose to go bare. I do not fault her for not wishing to accept too much from us in the beginning of our relationship. Her eyes roam from one human queen to another. They are all happy and well fed. I chose the dining hall so she could see with her own eyes that her people are welcome and well treated by my brethren. I watch her anxiety slowly click down a notch.

When Hero walks over with one huge platter of food, I am immediately envious because he will be sharing food from his plate with our new queen. I remember how her face drifted closer to his in the corridor outside the medical unit. Unless I am much mistaken, she was preparing to make the human kiss with him.

When Hero sits, she smiles up at him with such warmth that my heart stutters in my chest. He beams back at her and I know in my heart that if this queen is capable of overlooking Hero's many scars and plain features to see the kind and decent male inside, she will do the same for all of us.

As we eat, I find myself sneaking glances at the two of them as Hero brings a small bite of food to her mouth. He does all I once thought a breeder would do for our queen. If he can do such, surely the rest of us can as well. I freeze in my seat when she lifts a bite of food to his mouth and feeds him with her bare fingers.

Glancing around, I take out my sound dampener and set it in the middle of the table. Rather than pressuring her to ask her questions, I give her time to relax and enjoy her food. I don't know how I know but something tells me she is grateful for every bite she gets and every bit of attention she gets from her new protector. I begin to worry that I've misjudged the situation. Maybe human females really are only suited for one-to-one pairings.

Eventually, she eats her fill and feeds the rest to Hero. The older warrior luxuriates in her attention. Kane stands and walks over to a drink dispenser. I see him creating drinks the human queens are fond of drinking. The moment he sits down and distributes them, our new queen speaks.

"Now that I have you all together, I'd like to formally thank you for pulling me off that planet and for saving Trovena and her little ones."

I can't help but warm to her kind words. "We were pleased to be of service." Our queens of old were not thankful for our diligence. They saw it as a duty owed.

Human queens seem more objective in their assessment of us.

She seems to draw inwards into herself, bringing her hands into her lap before speaking again. "I wanted to ask who owns me at this point."

Blinking at her, I must admit that I did not expect that particular question. "You were rescued by an Arobian Peacekeeper."

"Is he the tall alien with the crystal implanted in his forehead?"

"It is actually an Arobian third eye, but yes, he is the one of whom I speak."

"Does that mean I belong to him for the time being?"

"No, he wishes to take possession of you in order to return you to your people. The Strovian whom you originally contracted with through the galactic bride registry quit his claim on you long ago in favor of taking an available bride. You are now free to accept another male or clade of males if you wish."

"So, the Arobian's not still after me?"

Hero speaks before I can respond. "The Peacekeeper still insists that you be turned over to him. I spoke with him while you cleansed this morning to alert him that you selected a protector and his services were no longer needed."

She looks hopefully up at her chosen protector. "What did he say to that?"

"He has spoken with your mother on Earth and they have determined you are to return. Once your family sees that you are well, you may select any clade you wish."

"That doesn't make any sense. Why would my family want me to travel such vast distances for no reason?"

I interject, "I believe everything happens for a reason, even if it is one we cannot readily grasp."

Kane joins the conversation. "Perhaps your family is untrusting and wishes to see with their own eyes that you are well and no one is forcing you to lie about such things."

Her delicate brow creases. "That might be the reason, but something seems off."

Leaning over the table, Jax makes a valid point. "You were missing for three long years and your galactic bride contract was voided. If I were your family, I might worry that without a proper contract you will be left at the mercy of whatever aliens accept you into their clade."

"My mother is pretty focused on things being done by the book."

"Do you not wish to visit with your family again?"

My question takes her by surprise. "Well, of course I would. But making a trip like that must take vast amounts of resources. Neither my family nor I have money to fund a trip home for me right now. Plus I don't like how that tall grabbed me and pulled me around like I was a criminal."

"If you wish it, we will agree to allow the Peacekeeper to escort us all to your home world. Once you are safely in the arms of your family, if you like us, we will establish a new contract through the galactic brides program to enable you to join our clade."

She is quiet for so long, I begin to wonder if she is going to refuse my offer. After glancing nervously up at Hero, she nods. "I'd love to get to know you all a little better. I really don't know anything about joining a clade, so maybe we could talk about that as we make the journey."

"The journey to Earth Major will take approximately four lunars from our location. The queen in command of this ship is Queen Daisy. She is intent upon visiting her home world to bring foodstuffs to humans in need. She also intends to allow more queens to board who wish to leave your dying world. Perhaps members of your family might wish to relocate to our new home world."

Queen Latisha's mouth falls open. Clearly she has not thought of such a thing before. I quickly assuage whatever fears I can imagine she might have. "Our clade would accept responsibility for whatever family you have. We are willing to care for your mother and any of your lankean hatch mates."

Hero murmurs, "Our clade leader means any of your beloved siblings."

Her eyes jump from me to him and back again. "What if something happens and I don't end up remaining with your clan?"

"This offer I make will be honored whether or not you choose to remain our queen."

Her expression is doubtful. I can't help being curious about her concerns. "Are you worried that I will not honor this offer to care for your lankean family or are you wary of joining my clade?"

Pressing herself closer to the warrior she gifted with a name of honor, she admits to having misgivings about both.

"I humbly suggest your concerns might be mitigated by getting to know us better, my queen."

"Your clan rescued me and you're doing what you can to keep me from being taken into custody again by that Arobian peacekeeper. Now you're offering to relocate my family and look after them as well. That's an offer no sane woman would turn down. I'm worried you're going to think the only reason I'm with you is because of all the favors."

"We care not the why of it, my queen. You are the loveliest female we have encountered among the human queens. You have shown your worth by being protective of your friend queen. We believe that demonstrated good character."

Hero speaks up. "We wish to get to know you better and are more than happy to extend the protection of our clade to those you hold dear."

A brief silence spins out as I try to better understand her reluctance. Kane is kind enough to supply the missing piece of information. "Human queens only mate if they grow love in their soul for the male. She worries that we are initiating a trade for what should be given freely."

My wings jerk hard, evidencing my surprise to be discussing the subject of love. "Though I see your growing fondness for our warrior, I never dared to hope you might grow such deep feelings for the rest of us. If this is a possibility, I wish to explore it in detail."

I see her shoulders relax and the hand she knotted in Hero's uniform sleeve loosens. Pride surges in my chest when I realize my words have hit their mark. Though I have lied to this pretty female, I am loath to admit that I did dare to hope she might grow a genuine liking or love for each of us. My com sounds and I reach for it without taking my eyes from her lovely face.

Queen Daisy's voice sounds from my com unit. "Hatch, I need to speak with your new queen. This peacekeeper will not leave until his concerns have been addressed."

I somehow manage to refrain from cursing under my breath. "Queen Latisha has agreed to return to Earth. However, she will remain under the protection of our clade for the duration of the trip. She wishes to speak with her family on Earth and I plan to make that happen shortly."

"Not that I doubt your word, but I'm going to need to hear her speak for herself."

Without additional prompting, our queen speaks up. "Everything Hatch said is true. I'm not overly fond of that peacekeeper, so if it's at all doable I'd like to stay with...um...my clade."

A thrill creeps up my spine that she's referred to us as her clade. Jax may harbor reservations about this queen being ours but I find myself liking her more by the moment.

"That's fine, but he insists upon seeing you in person to verify your safety."

I speak up on my queen's behalf. "Ask him to visit her in our clade quarters. We are headed there now."

"Roger that. If you need anything, don't hesitate to let us know."

Queen Latisha comes to her feet and we follow. Making our way to our clade's quarters, we take turns making polite conversation. She is curious about our ship, Queen Daisy and how we came to be in this sector of space. I expect her to ask to speak with Queen Daisy but she seems more fixated on the peacekeeper and what control, if any, he has over her. Truth be told I worry about this as well. He has galactic law on his side but I will wage the battle of a lifetime to keep her at our side if that is her wish.

My wings jerk with annoyance when I see the peacekeeper standing outside our quarters. Hero wraps her tighter to his body and her feet come to a stumbling stop for a moment before she moves again. My protective instincts rise so hard and fast, I think briefly of ripping him to shreds for causing her such worry. The others are as on guard as I am and together we have the upper hand.

I move forward to stand in front of my queen and Jax and Kane come up on either side. "Greetings, peacekeeper."

Without moving, he introduces himself. "My name is Peacekeeper Crovan."

"We are pleased to make your acquaintance. My name is Hatch and the other members of my clade are Jax, Kane and Hero, who's the one sheltering our queen under his wing."

"Greetings, clade and Latisha Brogan."

"Queen Daisy reports you wish to speak to our queen. We will allow this but you must not touch her or upset her in any way."

"I agree to those terms."

Voice prompting the door open, we all enter and take seats around my seating area. Latisha speaks before anyone else can begin. "Thank you for rescuing me, Peacekeeper Crovan. I was held captive for so long, I had lost hope of ever being free."

"Your mother posted a location verification request for her eldest child and I responded to her posting. I have been tracking your whereabouts for coming up on one solar cycle or what humans call a year."

Shock registers on our queen's face. "I can't imagine what my mother had to trade for such a lengthy investigation."

"I am not allowed to discuss the particulars of the contract she offered but I will say her payment is something I consider priceless."

My tail whips back and forth, hitting my leg with each sweep. The only trade that is truly priceless in the galaxy is for females. I'm incensed to think this desperate older queen traded one of Latisha's sisters for assistance rescuing our new mate. Intense dislike kicks in my gut for this peacekeeper.

"Well, I can't imagine what that might be. My new clan has offered to escort me to Earth, so you don't need to worry about that piece."

"The law has remanded you to my custody. I will be escorting you to Earth and collecting the bounty."

Seething, I break into their conversation. "You have already been informed that we will honor Queen Latisha's wish to travel under the protection of her clan."

His practically nonexistent chin lifts defiantly but his tone remains calm. "I refuse to relinquish custody of my charge until she is safely at her mother's side."

He sounds intractable but I will give no quarter on this issue. "Queen Latisha has claimed her clade. We refuse to relinquish her to you or any other male."

Though his face is not what one could consider expressive, I believe he is frowning. My mind scrambles to offer a compromise he might accept. "We have spare quarters adjacent to this room that we would be more than happy to offer the male who rescued our queen. It would provide a good vantage point for you to monitor our clade and our comings and goings. I have no objection to you visiting as often as you feel is necessary to ensure Queen Latisha's safety and wellbeing."

"I would have to speak with her mother before agreeing to such an offer, for she was quite specific about her daughter being isolated from all possible threats."

Our queen offers a suggestion to pave the way for a final solution. "Would it be possible to contact my mother and speak with her together? I could assure her that I feel more comfortable with my clan and let her know how Crovan went above and beyond to ensure my rescue from some really nasty captors."

Crovan's body relaxes and he agrees with an enthusiasm I did not expect. "Yes, I wish you to speak well of me to your mother. If she agrees, I have no objections to you remaining with your clade under my watchful eye."

Before anyone can change their minds, I voice prompt our large viewing screen. Crovan enters the twelve-digit alphanumeric code to connect with our queen's family. The channel clicks for what seems like an endless amount of time before a frail queen's upper torso appears. If I had thought Queen Latisha was malnourished, it is nothing compared to the female who appears in front of us. She looks like a hollowed out and frailer version of our queen. Her serviceable clothing is threadbare and her hair dry and brittle. I'm too stunned to speak, as is the rest of my clade.

Peacekeeper Crovan's voice drops as their eyes meet. "I secured the release of your daughter as promised."

The woman's eyes tear up slightly and she blinks, I think trying to keep them from spilling down her face. "Bring her to me and I will fulfil the terms of our contract."

Finally, Latisha manages to speak. "What happened, mother?" She doesn't need to point out that the woman looks extremely emaciated, for that is obvious to everyone in the room.

The woman looks uncomfortable. She smooths one hand down her thin stomach as she gathers her thoughts. I'm guessing she is choosing her words carefully, trying to decide what is appropriate to share with her daughter who is not looking much better herself. "Things here have taken a turn for the worst. We thought inflation was a thing of the past, but come to find out it's alive and well on planet Earth."

Crovan opts out of the conversation, electing to get onto his handheld. I don't know what he's doing but it's disrespectful to ignore the suffering of others.

I'm vaguely aware that his long skinny fingers are scrolling quickly through menus but I can't see his screen clearly enough to know what he's doing.

Latisha's mother continues, "There is more separation than ever before between those with means and the rest of us." Pausing briefly to stare at her daughter, her expression displays a mixture of urgency and pain. "You must come home, Latisha. It's the only way."

Our queen immediately acquiesces to her mother's desperate plea. "I will get there as soon as possible. Will you be alright until then?"

Her eyes drop down to the bottom of the screen to see what I assume is a private message and her shoulders relax. Nodding her head, her eyes fill with unshed tears. "Yes. We will be fine. I've been told you chose a clan from among the Draconians. Is that true?"

We all move closer and she introduces us one by one. This is normally a solemn occasion for a newly formed clade. It galls me that the peacekeeper is here to witness what should be a private moment.

Our new queen mother looks at each of us in turn and appears pleased by what she sees. "Welcome to our family, gentlemen. I wish you all happiness and a wealth of children."

My chest loosens a bit. If we can convince our new queen to accept us more than just for appearance's sake, I will be well satisfied. Instead of allowing my worry to slip out, I reply warmly, "Your daughter will be the center of our world. Rest assured we will protect her with our lives and see she is well loved and respected."

Latisha's curious eyes flash to me and for a brief second I think she might object to my words. Instead she reassures her mother the best she can under the circumstances. "I really am safe now. Peacekeeper Crovan tracked me through three galaxies and fought off some really awful species to free me. Thank you for filing the missing person's report on me. If you hadn't done that, I'd still be trapped in a dirty cage."

Her mother's expression changes to one of gratitude and awe as her eyes find the peacekeeper. He's now all ears and doesn't take his eyes off her. Our queen mother speaks to him with genuine warmth. "Crovan, I want you to know that I will be forever in your debt."

"I do not require your undying gratitude, Margaret. I just want what is due me."

"It will be my honor to deliver on my promises."

A blue tinge crawls up the Arobian's skin, until his third eye is practically glowing with what I assume is happiness, though it could be embarrassment or even lust. Latisha's mother seems pleased with the exchange she made with this Arobian.

When the screen goes blank, I speak up on behalf of our new queen mother. It tears at my heart to see her so impoverished. "With your permission, Queen Latisha, I would fill your mother's account with enough credits to see her easily through the next few lunars until our arrival."

Before she can speak Crovan comes to his feet. "I have taken care of that already. You will not speak about this to her, for she would find it humiliating."

My gaze shifts to our queen. She nods, turning to speak to the peacekeeper. "My mother would abhor taking charity. She'd do it if it meant keeping body and soul together but she'd be really embarrassed. Thank you for putting some credits into her account without bringing it up to her. That was real nice of you."

"I have tracked you far and wide. We were out of contact for several lunars. We are only now within com range of your planet once more. I would not have allowed her to go without."

Latisha's expression turns perplexed. The suspicion grows stronger in my mind that this peacekeeper has more than a casual interest in my queen's family. It bears monitoring.

After we discuss the peacekeeper visiting again in the morning, we all say our goodbyes and Crovan reluctantly takes his leave of us. Jax heads to our auxiliary quarters to clear out our belongings to make space for Crovan and Kane heads back to his assignment. I'm pleased to have time alone with Hero and our queen.

LATISHA

By the time most of them have cleared out, my head is spinning. So much has happened in twenty-four hours that I'm having a hard time catching my breath. Coming to my feet, I can't help but pace. My mother looked horrible and insinuated she needed me to come home. There's something going on between her and that peace-keeper and it worries me. None of my siblings are quite old enough to sign up for the galactic brides program and I can't imagine what she would have had to trade to get that tall to track my whereabouts for almost a complete year.

As if intuiting my worries, Hatch speaks. "Perhaps your mother found something of value on your home world, something only valued by Arobians. That would explain how she engaged his services."

Stopping in my tracks, I see both Hatch and Hero standing as well. It's clear I'm worrying them by pacing. Rubbing my hands down my uniform, I walk back over to the seating area. The day's not half over and I'm already mentally and physically exhausted. "It would have had to be something extremely valuable." Before we can get tangled up in another exhausting conversation, I ask, "Would it be possible for me to lay down for a bit? My head is spinning and we've not even talked about the us piece of this puzzle."

Hero moves to my side and slips his wing around my back. He smells amazing and my brain goes on a little vacation remembering how he looked naked. His tail snakes around my leg and I move closer without meaning to. "Do you wish me to stay by your side?"

The answer to that question is a big yes. However, if his big sexy half-naked body is stretched out beside me that's all I'll be thinking about. Shaking my head, I explain, "Right now, I need some quiet time by myself to think about my life choices."

If his feelings are hurt, he doesn't show it. Instead he steers me to the back of the room and into the room with the huge bed. I now realize it's sized to hold their entire clan. Then I realize something else. I'm the 'plus one' in the clan sleeping arrangement. I'll be damned if it doesn't look like we'll all fit in the damned thing. Trying to make myself feel some kind of way is not working. Rather than angry, I'm curious and slightly aroused. It hits me hard and fast that if it were remotely possible physically, I'd claim this entire clan. Hero pulls back the luxuriously soft blankets and I crawl into the bed with my mind filled with images of all of them naked and willing to do whatever I say. When Hero leans over to pull the blankets up, I can't help but assuage my curiosity. "If I joined your clan, who would be in charge when it comes to mating?"

Tugging the blanket up around my shoulders his expression softens. "Queens are in command of a clade at all times. You mate only when you like, with whichever male you want and how you like. It is our honor to serve you."

Grabbing him by the front of his uniform, I pull him down and slightly to the side. My lips drift over his neck and I lick around the shell of his ear before whispering. "On my home world licking is a way of claiming. It means you're now mine and no other woman can touch you."

He goes stiff as a board and for one endless moment I think he's going to object. Instead he turns his head and licks around the shell of my ear as well. Suddenly, I know why he went stiff. Having someone's tongue on that sensitive skin sends a bolt of heat right down to my girly bits. Just when I'm thinking of pulling the sexy man into bed with me, he straightens. His expression is pure happiness with an overlay of heat. "You will not regret the choice you make today, my queen."

Feeling emboldened by his response, words pour out of my mouth before I really consider what I'm saying. "Tell the rest of your clan that I'm interviewing males for my own clan and they are first on my list of males I wish to speak with."

His eyes grow large. "You wish to have a clan of your own?"

My eyes get heavy as I relax back into the soft bed. "Sure, why not? With a clan there would be more protection, more companionship and more hotness." As I drift off to sleep it occurs to me that perhaps women are not allowed to be clan leaders. If so, I'll have to settle for joining their clan.

## Hero

I stand vigil until I know she is sleeping soundly then slip out to speak with my clade. They are thrilled that I have been formally selected for mating by our new queen and most interested in this ritual acceptance by licking.

"It is not unpleasant." When they don't respond, I add, "I found it to be quite enjoyable."

"Humans have strange customs but I must admit this one piques my interest."

Hatch's response means he's open to exploring human customs and that eases my mind. "I felt certain you would all comply with our new queen's demands. Unfortunately, she is not like the queens we have known. She rarely makes her wishes known verbally and usually phrases them as a question or request. It was difficult to acclimate to at first."

Kane interjects, "Human queens are less demanding by nature than Draconian queens. The breeders learned rather quickly to pay attention to their facial expressions and body language. They wear their feelings for all to see."

Jax chuckles as he joins the conversation for the first time. "I have helped care for them over the last few lunars. I do not believe I've seen even one of them wear the neutral expression of a warrior."

Warriors are taught from an early age to maintain a blank expression, no matter the circumstances. Jax is correct in pointing out that human females' faces are very expressive. "The greater issue for me has been her expression and mood shifting so quickly that I have a difficult time keeping up."

"Being mated to a human queen will be a challenge in many ways. However, there are many rewards to be earned if we are diligent and act with honor."

Jax teases, "Perhaps we will earn names of honor. I for one would love for our queen to look to me in her time of need the way she does her Hero."

Kane nods. "Her easy acceptance of Hero has sealed

the deal for me. If the option is still open, I wish to join your clan."

Hatch's hand goes out to rest on his shoulder. "Welcome to the House of Citron. With a queen maker among our ranks we can be assured of having an abundance of young."

I quickly point out, "That will only be true if she accepts Kane into our clan and if she considers him worthy to breed. Also, I do not believe there is a House of Citron anymore. If there is, it will shortly be dissolved in favor of a new clan."

Hatch and Kane's heads snap around to stare at me so quickly I worry that I have offended. I explain before they become even more annoyed. "Queen Latisha wishes to establish a clan of her own rather than join with our clan." Their wings jerk in astonishment, much as mine did when she told me her wishes. Swallowing thickly, I continue. "Queen Latisha informed me that I am chosen and that no other female may touch what is hers. She also wishes me to communicate to you that she is on the lookout for clan members and wishes to interview you all before any others."

A long silence spins out as we all think about the implications of being in a clan led by a female. Hatch is our leader and Queen Latisha does not seem dominant enough to lead a clan of four Draconian males. This is obvious to all present.

Finally Kane speaks. His voice is full of confidence. "This changes nothing but semantics. We all know queens rule their clades. We also know there is usually a male tasked with seeing that her wishes are carried out. Hatch will clearly still be running the day to day operations of our clade. He will be expected to make all the decisions unimportant enough to bother a queen with as well. Are we in agreement?"

I find myself nodding practically before he finishes speaking. "I will be responsible for the security of our clade."

Jax is warming quickly to the idea of joining with this queen. "Being a healer, I will ensure the health and physical wellbeing of our clade."

"Being a breeder, I'm knowledgeable about how to best support a queen and care for our young. Though I have no wish to give up my position as a warrior, I will do whatever becomes necessary to best serve our clade." Kane seems torn between being a breeder to a soft human queen and enjoying his position among the ranks of warriors. I find myself wishing we could switch places, for I have no wish to be anyplace other than at my queen's side.

Hatch nods his agreement. "We all have our roles to play. We need to each spend time alone with her, otherwise we have no hope of distinguishing ourselves."

Kane objects to Hatch's reasoning. "I believe that because she has experienced abuse by her captors we should be careful to ensure she feels safe. Perhaps we should all go about our normal routine for a few days, leaving Hero alone with her. When he is certain she is acclimating, we will take turns spending the day with the two of them until she is comfortable being alone with each of us."

"Agreed. Since we are all sharing quarters now, we can visit as a group in the evenings. Though she might be anxious, she needs to become comfortable with the clade structure."

This sounds like a good plan to me. It's reassuring that we are all of like minds regarding courting our queen. "I will speak with our queen and explain our plan."

"Hero, I know you are sensitive to upsetting our new queen but I believe the less we involve her in the planning the less anxious she will become."

Hatch is sorely mistaken if he believes my loyalty to our queen comes secondary to the wishes of the clade. "I refuse to knowingly deceive my queen. I wish you all to understand that I have been chosen, so my first loyalty will always be to my queen. The difference between sound planning and manipulation is small. I wish to stay on the right side of this issue."

Hatch pins me with an assessing gaze. None of the others dare to speak, for I am going against the wishes of our clade leader. After much apparent thoughtful consideration, Hatch speaks. "Since you have been chosen and we have not, I have to believe there is a reason for that. Perhaps it is because you know our queen's heart better than me. On this issue I will rely upon your good judgment. However, do not think I will relinquish my role so docilely in all matters."

His tone isn't angry or harsh but I can tell he's concerned about being robbed of his status and function in our family unit. "I can't say any of us are interested in stepping into your role, Hatch. I am but a simple warrior. Fighting and protecting is what I'm good at. Our queen expects me to be only what I am."

His wings relax and I realize he was very close to unfurling then in a display of dominance. Bringing my fist up to rub my chest, I realize provoking my clade leader distresses me. I do not like this feeling of being at odds with him but I will do what must be done to ensure that every decision is resolved in my queen's favor.

"Jax, did you bring the suppressors?"

"Yes. You spoke and I obeyed."

I frown at the fawning little fool. Jax is a good male but

he curries favor when there is no need. I know what Hatch is going to say before he opens his mouth. Our new queen will want to test our sexual skills but now is not the time to overwhelm her with young. The suppressors will keep us from releasing our mating scent and protect against conception.

"I am chosen. Such decisions are now for my queen to make." I hate being oppositional but I cannot allow Hatch to overstep his bounds.

Instead of being upset, his expression flushes with pleasure. "You are correct, Hero. Your queen must be given the opportunity to choose when and where to breed all her males. We will use suppressors until we are chosen then we will also follow our queen's lead."

This situation is getting more complicated by the moment. "I wish you to leave my injection in case my queen wishes more time before breeding me."

Jax walks over and hands me a tiny disposable hypospray. When I take it from his hands, he grasps my shoulders. I glance up and see his expression is one of approval. Something loosens in my chest. Being chosen before my closest friend is more difficult than I would have imagined.

THE OTHERS HAVE LEFT AND HAPPINESS FILLS MY heart to be alone, watching over my queen once more. She looks so small and delicate sleeping with her long pale hair spilling over the fluffy squares. Memories of her smiling at me and the sound of her voice fill my head.

I step closer when she moves in her sleep, worried that she might be having another bad dream. Rather than thrashing around, she jerks awake and lays staring at me. I watch her blink, as though trying to focus her eyes.

When she smiles at me, I step closer and sit on the edge of the sleeping platform. Approaching this queen is allowed because I am chosen. She moves to sit up and stretches her arms over her head. She's wearing only the thin covering we sometimes wear under our uniforms. The pale grey fabric clings to her curves, enticing me to drink in the beauty before me. The grey in her clothing brings out the grey in her eyes.

"You're made of eyes today, Hero."

A smile comes unbidden to my face at the light and playful tone of her voice. "I would normally guard my eyes, but since I am chosen, enjoying the sight of whatever you choose to reveal is permitted."

Sliding her legs over the opposite side of the bed, she murmurs softly, "You guys sure have a lot of rules. I don't know if I'll ever keep them all straight." Turning to face me, she lifts her shirt and slowly tears it over her head. Standing with the thin garment in her hands, she seems to be almost daring me to look. And look I do. For a long moment she allows my gaze to roam over her naked torso.

My mouth goes dry at the sight of her pale soft body, the gentle swell of her breasts and the way her hair falls over her shoulders. Just when I am certain that I will be reprimanded, she drops the fabric. It wafts silently to the floor and her hand comes to the front of the undergarment covering what I most wish to see. I'm riveted by her slight form. She bends, slowly moving the fabric down her legs. When she straightens again, revealing short curly hairs decorating the top of her pretty slit, I feel like this is something forbidden but I can't take my eyes from her body.

Before thinking, I rasp, "You are the most beautiful person in the 'verse to me."

She smiles and steps her feet out of the clothing she just removed. I stand, making myself ready to serve as she commands. Though it sounds like an ocean roaring in my ears, I remember that I must tell her about the suppressor. Before I can explain about that, she speaks.

"I'm in charge when we're naked, right?"

I nod enthusiastically. "Queens command and males obey in all things."

"Good. How about you get out of that uniform and let me have a look at all of you."

"You wish me to bare my warrior's body for inspection?

I did not think human queens inspected their males for flaws."

She makes a gesture with one hand that seems to be a prompt. Not wishing to be rejected I pull open my uniform top and begin shoving it down my legs. Truth be told, I wish to be naked and in the same room with my queen. It puts us one step closer to mating.

I don't take my eyes off my queen as I disrobe. The Gods only know when such an opportunity will present itself again. Therefore, I will look my fill while I can. Something nags at the back of my mind but I can't remember. I was meant to do something. Just as it is coming to me, her feminine voice interrupts my train of thought.

"Humans don't inspect each other for flaws."

"I am glad for that, for your protector has many."

"You're looking pretty damn good from where I'm standing."

"I am confused. You were wary of us and now you are... the opposite of wary."

She laughs and the joyful sound fills my soul with pure happiness. I stand proudly, as naked as my queen, allowing her to look her fill. Her expression is approving and it makes me feel like I am enough.

"I slept on it and woke up in a different frame of mind. I've spent the last three years being forced to do someone else's bidding. Your clan is giving me an opportunity to make decisions for myself and I've decided I deserve a treat."

I'm hopelessly lost. Human queens consider sweets and tokens of affection treats, not huge scarred warriors. "Looking at me cannot be a treat for your eyes. Nothing about me is worthy of a queen."

"If I'm truly in charge, I have your very first order. From now out, you will respect yourself the way you respect me."

Her words touch my soul. She wishes for me to see my true worth as a male. "If this is important to you, I will try. To ask such a thing tells me you may not understand the difference between a precious queen and a simple warrior."

She climbs onto the bed and moves to the center. Sitting back on her own legs in a position that cannot possibly be comfortable, she speaks in earnest. "If being a slave has taught me anything, it's that I can't judge my value by what others think." Holding out her arms she looks down. "My body has scars, yet you do not think less of me."

I try to hide a smile. "Those are not scars. They are marks of beauty."

Watching her run her hands seductively around each breast, I'm captivated by the long thin lines that run from the tip back, disappearing into her creamy flesh. They accentuate the plumpness of each beautiful breast. I wish to run my tongue down each tiny line.

She holds out both hands and I move forward into her warm embrace. He breasts mash against my chest when she wraps her arms around my neck and pulls me to her. "You are soft, my queen."

"Call me Tisha. Touch anyplace you like."

I jerk in her arms, surprised to be given such liberties. Reaching around, I run my hands up her back, thrilling at the feel of her warm skin. Everything about this female lures me in, makes me want to handle her with care and protect her. That something tugs at the back of my mind again but whatever I was supposed to do slips away when her hands land on my cock.

I pull back to watch her hands sliding back and forth. Her two pale hands moving over my large rough scarred cock looks almost obscene. I close my eyes because the pleasure she gives is almost too much. Realizing this may be my one and only opportunity to mate, I force them open again because I don't want to miss a moment of this visual. "Forgive me, my queen."

"Whatever are you apologizing for, Hero?"

"I should not have permitted myself to get hard without your approval."

"Hell's bells, handsome. I consider that a compliment. It means you're really attracted to me."

"I am more than attracted to you, my sweet queen. This rough warrior now lives only to see you happy and safe. I will one day give my life to protect you. On that day you will select another to take my place. It is the way of our people."

Tugging my cock closer her expression turns annoyed. "Talking about dying for me might not be the great turn on you think it is."

"I am your protector." I don't talk about dying but surely that is the purpose of a protector. Does she not know?

Reaching down to stroke my testis, she murmurs, "You can't protect me if you're dead, my handsome warrior."

The truth of her words makes me reassess everything I thought I knew about being a warrior and a protector. She wishes me to take great care with myself in order that I might be around to protect her for longer. The queens of old saw warriors as highly expendable. Therefore, warriors came to think of ourselves as such.

Her hands drift from my cock to frame my face. Tilting my head up to look into my eyes, she asks sincerely, "You want this, right? Sex, I mean."

"My cock is as hard as it's ever been and mating with you is my one desire at the moment." Speaking of mating jars my brain and I remember in a flash what I was meant to talk about with her. "I should warn you that..."

One hand comes out and she presses her fingers to my lips in gesture meant to shut me up. "Is having sex with you going to harm me or you?"

With her fingers still firmly covering my lips I shake my head once.

"Then I want less conversation and more lovemaking."

"But I am supposed to..."

"Nope, not listening to any more of your drivel about how you're gonna end up dead or you're not good-looking enough or the planets aren't in proper alignment for us to mate. You want me and I want my sexy treat. Come here and kiss me."

I'm thrilled at her words. This pale queen wants me as much as I want her. I have never been thought of as a treat before. She reaches out with one hand and pulls me down. I forget all about the suppressor, for my queen clearly wishes to breed me this night.

The moment we are face-to-face she makes the human kiss with me. I have seen mated males do this many times and always wished to experience it for myself. This day will live in my memory as the day I was introduced to the pleasures of being with a female by my beautiful human queen.

When our lips connect, my world spins for a brief moment. Nothing has ever felt this good. When my lips part slightly, she slides her tongue into my mouth. She must be seeking my tongue because there is nothing else in my mouth. I slide my tongue against hers and it is most sensuous experience I have ever known. I freeze for a brief moment, and before I know it, my arms are around her and I'm drawing her close. Rather than object to my brazen handling, she makes a tiny needy sound that is all female.

She moves back until I am leaning over her, gazing down upon all her loveliness. She's still in charge but allows me to take the position of dominance. This beautiful creature saw me as worthy of mating and chose me from among the many. For that I will be forever grateful. If I am not much mistaken her submissive pose is her way of offering herself to me. Being the greedy male that I am, I will eagerly take all that she offers this night.

## Latisha

Laying here staring up at this gorgeous man, I can't believe that I got naked and jumped right into bed with an alien I hardly know, especially after I've suffered so much deprivation and abuse at the hands of aliens over the last three years. If I'm counting the hardships on Earth before I left, I've been lacking even the basic necessities of life for a lot longer than three years. Hero makes me feel safe. More importantly, he looks at me like I'm beautiful and desirable. It heals some of the hurt I feel deep inside.

Accepting Hero and wallowing in his adoration is the first time I've ever made a selfish decision just for me. I want this man like I've never wanted anything else in my life. He's kind, attentive and seems like a genuinely nice person. I don't mind that he's an alien. His differences are part of what attracts me to him.

He smells amazing and I want to lick every square inch of his body. There's only one thing stopping me. The way he's leaning over me with his wings unfurled is breathtaking. He looks for all the world like a conquering god. And it's turning my insides to jelly. Whatever is going on between us, I want more of it. Laying claim to him the way I did was totally reckless but I feel our connection all the way down to my bones.

His hand comes up to touch my face in an almost reverent caress. The tips of his fingers feel rough against my skin. The more he touches the more I want. I wiggle closer, placing one leg on either side of his body. His eyes don't go straight for the apex of my thighs. No, my new man's a gentleman. He kisses me like he owns me and I freakin' love it. My nipples are hard and I'm wetter than I've ever been. For a woman who's been through a lot, my libido has come back with a roar.

His lips skate over and down the side of my neck. He's nipping at me with those sharp fangs, being really careful not to break my skin. His tongue comes out to lick each place he nibbles and it's driving me mad. When he moves down to my breasts, he's almost hesitant. Tilting his head up to look me in the eyes, he swallows thickly. "Am I permitted to touch your bountiful breasts?"

*My bountiful breasts?* Oh man, I can't help but laugh at his phrasing. It causes him to flush and his wings jerk back. His face settles into that blank expression I hate so much. I didn't mean to embarrass him. I make up for it by cupping his face with both my hands and rubbing my thumbs across his cheeks. He loosens up again and I answer his absurdly phrased question. "Yes. I love having my breasts touched. For human females they're a sensitive place and touching them spikes our arousal."

His lips curve up slightly, reminding me exactly how handsome he is. "Good, I wish my queen to be soaked with need and begging for my cock."

"I'm lovin' that dirty mouth." Teasing him causes a full-on smile to break open his face and he goes immediately to work discovering what turns me on. He's a smart and resourceful man. It takes him no time at all to figure out how to make my nipples stand out more than I ever thought they could.

His amazing scent is making me want to run my nose over his skin. Instead I grab the two fat horns on each side of his head and steer his face downward to where I want his mouth most. He goes almost eagerly. I'm stunned when he pets my pubic hair and runs his fingers through it before glancing up at me.

I give him the same helpful nod I did before and he rubs his cheek against it. I feel something wrapping around one leg, twining around my knee. It's his long thick tail. I'm fucking fascinated by his tail. My breath hitches when it snakes around my leg tighter, pulling it back and out of his way. I quickly move my other leg back as well, giving his broad shoulders room to work.

His voice is raspy and deep when he speaks. "You smell delicious, my queen."

I don't correct him about the name thing cause I'm too flippin' excited to experience the pleasure he's keen on dishing out tonight. Right now this handsome man is my whole world. When his mouth makes contact my entire body lights up with pleasure. His tongue strokes a long, wet trail from one end to the other, stopping only long enough to dip into my core. A lusty noise comes from the back of his throat and his licking becomes rougher and faster. When he finds my clit, my eyes roll back in my head with sheer pleasure. He experiments until he figures out I like the direct stimulation on top of my clit, light and fast. Once he has me figured out, he's relentless.

My hands are still on his horns and I can't even process the fact that my new guy has horns. Suddenly, there is a finger inside my soaked channel and then another, stroking to find the right spot. I explode when his lips wrap around my clit and he sucks for the first time. I come screaming his name. Hero doesn't stop until I pull him off me using his horns. By then I'm a limp noodle.

His expression is a mixture of smug satisfaction and pent up sexual aggression. I'm intrigued by that and suddenly anxious to feel his cock inside me. I reach out with one leg and wrap it around right beneath his ass and jerk him forward. His eyes go perfectly round. "You wish my cock?"

It's clear the poor man couldn't be more shocked. I try to think of something more shocking and a brilliant idea pops into my head. "I want your tail first."

Sure enough he jerks and his wings click out another thirty degrees. Looking him over, I realize his body is like a sensual playground for a woman like me. He's good at all the things women like. Snatching him up was the best decision I ever made.

He doesn't move. Our eyes are still locked in a stare that neither of us can seem to break. His dark eyes are hauntingly beautiful. I can tell this man has been through some things. In this we are the same. Two reckless lost souls colliding in the night.

I feel his tail release my leg and slide between my thighs from behind. The tip is thick but blunted. When it slips through my folds, colliding with my overly sensitive clit, my eyes drop down to his lips. As if he can read my mind, Hero leans down to take my lips in a breathtakingly dominant kiss. He takes and I glory in giving. Tasting myself on his lips isn't offensive. It only ratchets up my level of arousal.

He pulls back and we look down to see the blunt tip of his tail hovering near my core. I'm embarrassed by how wet I am for him. He doesn't have to do anything but wait for my arousal to drip down and cover the tip of his tail. When I look at his face my stomach flips at his fascinated and lust-filled expression.

When he's wet, his eyes lift to mine for a brief second as if assessing my willingness. My Hero must find what he's looking for because he spears me with the blunt tip and I moan shamelessly in pleasure. Enthralled with my response, he thrusts in and out several times before I brush it away in favor of his cock.

Rather than moving over me, he rolls us, putting me on top. His tail doesn't seem to want to play nice. It's wrapped around my hip and trying to get between my legs. His thick stiff cock bangs against my ass, reminding me that he's gotten very little in the way of sexual pleasure from me at this point. I consider using my mouth on him but we're both too needy. Seeing him lying there with his wings spread out on either side of his body gazing up at me with such need makes me want to reward my generous lover. He helps lift me and I grab his cock, placing the tip at my slick core.

Putting both hands on his chest, I slowly sink down. It's slow going, even after being stretched by his fingers and that gorgeous tail. Something about being fucked by his tail feels deliciously dirty. I must be a bad girl cause I can't wait to do that again. There's a bit of burn but his cock fills me up to the point of feeling stuffed.

Hero's hands are still grasping my waist but his arms are trembling. At this point we're both a hot mess. I lean forward and lift myself slightly and then drop back down. We both make sounds of pleasure. After the first few up and down motions, Hero takes over. We settle into a nice rhythm, with each downward stroke becoming more powerful until he's slamming me down on his cock with some force. I may be crazy but the pleasure with a tiny hint of pain is flipping all the right switches for me. My head falls back as the most powerful orgasm of my life rips through my body. A second later he slams me down one last time and holds me in place. Hero's body seizes up and he begins pouring his seed into me. It surprises me that I can feel it but I can't think straight anymore.

My back hits the soft bedding and he looks down at me with concern, his hand coming out to move a strand of hair from my face. Looking into his dark eyes, my heart fills with love. When I smile, he returns it.

"I thought I might have broken you, my sweet queen."

"You gave me the best sex of my entire life." Not that I've had much sex but I don't tell him that part.

He beams, pride etched on every inch of his scarred face. "I never thought having a precious queen would be this wonderful. Thank you for choosing me."

His hand is still beside my head so I turn my face into his palm. "Do you think we should make a clan of two?"

His happy expression falls immediately away, making me wish I hadn't spoiled our perfect moment. He responds tightly, "If that is your wish, it will be so."

"Tell me the advantages of a clan." I've already thought a little about it, so his response turns out to be a mixture of things I've considered and things that would have never occurred to me.

"My clan is well configured to care for a queen. Hatch is smart and got us into positions that better suit our interests and synchronized our schedules to enable us to spend time together. He is well thought of and I feel confident in his leadership."

I grin at his attempt to talk his clan leader up to me. "He sounds like a real asset."

Perhaps intuiting my attempt at meeting him halfway,

he nods before continuing. "Jax is the best healer of his class. He can dress battle wounds and oversee the hatching of our young."

I roll right past that not so subtle difference between our species, thinking that maybe that's just what they call birthing. "Humans hold doctors in high esteem, especially competent ones. We'd be lucky to have a trained healer in our clan."

Suddenly, his face lights up. "Jax is more than just a healer. He's lighthearted, funny and likes to challenge us in games of strategy. He, above all the others, is my closest friend."

"I can't wait to get to know him. If he's as much fun as you say he'll be the oil that keeps the rest of us from taking life too seriously."

His expression turns adoring at my open acceptance of his dear friend. If I was expecting any jealousy, I'd have been dead wrong. He's eager for me to accept his other clan members. "Tell me about Kane."

His expression shutters for an instant and he takes a moment to choose his words. When the words don't come, he rolls over onto his back and stares at the ceiling. His behavior isn't exactly an unreserved endorsement.

I roll onto my side and prop my head on my upturned hand. Instead of rushing him, I give him a moment to decide what he wants to say. He looks over at me for a split second before rolling over to face me.

"Most of my body scars are from our former queen. The warriors who were largest could bear the most abuse in her opinion."

My eyes skate over the multitude of scars and I realize an awful lot of them look like slashes. Fighting back tears, I whisper, "Tell me everything."

"Draconian queens are ruthless and often play one male off against another. They enjoy dealing pain the way human queens enjoy dealing pleasure." He pauses for a brief moment and his wings draw up tightly behind him. "In the times before we came to this dimension, males were divided into two classes, warriors and breeders. Breeders were reserved for the luxury of a queen's bed and served at her pleasure. Warriors were considered highly expendable."

"That sucks."

"My story is not over. There are differences in the way we create young."

I'm vaguely aware that Draconian males become with child when they are exposed to the pheromones of compatible female. It dawns on me that he could be carrying my young even now.

He continues, "Breeders carry many young, while we warriors only spawn one to three. Therefore breeders became companions to our ruthless queens while warriors were rarely exposed to enough female pheromones to conceive. Draconian males have a strong desire to continue our lines."

I can guess the rest. "Naturally there was conflict between breeders and warriors."

"That would be a gross understatement, my Tisha. The conflict was constant and could become extreme. Queens were tasked with settling disputes and they always defended the wishes of their breeders."

"If you think I'm going to let Kane hang around and sow discord, you've got another think coming."

He shakes his head, looking miserable. "The problem is me. I cannot find it in my heart to trust the young breeder, though he has not given me cause to doubt his intentions. Though he is younger and by all reports he is of good character, I am a stubborn old fool when it comes to trusting them."

I scoot closer, snuggling up to his chest. "We'll find our way through this together. I won't make any decisions unless we both feel comfortable about it."

His wing comes around to cover us and he tucks my head under his chin. "I have no right to take away your right to choose."

"You're not. I'm still in control, but I trust your judgment. We'll decide on whether to accept the breeder together." I feel him relax as I rub my cheek against his hard chest. My poor Hero's untrusting heart must be a weight for him to bear. Sharing the burden will surely lighten his load.

HATCH

Making it through the night was difficult knowing the suppressor was taking away my right to breed our queen while at the same time Hero was spawning with her. Surely this is not how taking a queen should be. Should not the clan leader spawn first? I snort a laugh at my own train of thought, for I well know there are no rules when it comes to mating human queens. They chose who they like with no regard for status or breed. Our lovely queen chose as her first an older warrior, one the other clans passed over because they thought his many scars and rough manner would drive prospective queens away. Jax and I were lucky enough to see his worth and I am glad for it.

Still, our clan quarters are filled with the sweet smell of mating scents. Normally Draconian males hate the smell of another male's mating scent. However, I discovered something interesting this morning. Hero's scent mixed with the scent of our queen is almost delightful. Perhaps it is knowing he serviced her in our stead that makes it bearable, for I would not wish a queen to lay needy in her bed while there are willing males about to see to her needs.

I suspect both Jax and Kane feel the same way because it means we will soon have young in our clade. If I am correct, that would explain their contented mood and the fact that I am hearing no complaints. Even now they work in companionable silence to set up a virtual feast for our new queen. Kane secured warming devices from the ship's kitchen and they are warming and preparing our food to ensure everything is at proper temperatures.

We are all excited to see our queen this morning. I hope she is relaxed and well loved. I fuss over the seating area, draping a luxurious throw over the edge of a settee and moving the fluffy squares queens are so smitten with about to show to their best advantage.

All our hard work is rewarded when Queen Latisha wanders out of the clan resting space with a smile on her face. The smile seems genuine and does not falter when she see us. Hero outfitted her in a pale formfitting suit that clings to her few curves. She needs to be fed to bloom into her lush form like the other queens my people have rescued. I try not to dwell on the swell of her breasts but it is difficult.

The lilting laughter in her voice catches my notice when she teasingly chides us. "My eyes are up here, guys."

My wings jerk when I realize we were all likely staring at her form rather than showing proper respect. We all immediately drop to our knees.

I see her coming to a stuttering stop in my peripheral vision. "What are you doing? Is it time to pray? Wait, I can figure this out. We all pray before we eat, right?"

I speak dutifully. "We bow out of respect." Daring to lift my eyes, I add quickly, "And we apologize for not guarding our eyes in the presence of a queen."

"Are you serious?" She wrinkles her nose in way that might be described as adorable. I think she is bemused by my answer. "Get up, all of you. This being on your knees business is going to have to stop if we're going to be a clan." Her expression turns mischievous for a moment but she gets herself under control.

An image of me kneeling before her naked form performing the Revidian comes to mind and I can't help but wonder if she wasn't thinking the same thing. I come quickly to my feet and reply glibly, "We will save the kneeling for mating. Come, my queen, we have prepared food for you this morning."

Though she moves forward, she reminds us that her chosen one is not yet out of the shower. "Hero will be along when he finishes his shower."

I pull out a chair, "We will have our morning drink while we wait for him." Kane hands her a steaming cup of tea we make from leaves grown on our new home world and we wait breathlessly to see if she likes the blend.

Once again we are rewarded with her approval when she takes a sip. Her face lights up and her voice increases in pitch slightly. "This tastes really nice. It reminds me of a mint tea my mother made as a child."

I am certain she does not know it but this is the highest compliment that can be given in our culture. Jax's head comes up and it is clear he's pleased. I explain smoothly, "Our healer experimented with many combinations of leaves to create the perfect morning beverage. He even tried them out on the queens aboard this vessel to find this particular mix. Of course when they are in the medical bay he has a bit of a captive audience."

She laughs at my gentle jibe and everyone relaxes.

"Did you sleep well last night, Queen Latisha?"

Taking another sip of her steaming brew, she sighs with pleasure. "I did sleep well. Hero was a wonderful bed partner. He's a bit rough and tumble, so if I'm not walking right today that would be why."

Kane chokes on his drink, clearly shocked that she's so bold about her compliments. I press my lips together to keep from laughing but Jax isn't so disciplined. A surprised noise escapes his throat. Our queen chuckles. "If we're going to be a clan, I guess we have to learn to talk about the s word."

It takes me a minute to realize the word for intimacy begins with an s in her language. I supply helpfully, "Draconians are open about all forms of breeding."

Kane chimes in, "Humans don't care for the word breeding. Many of the queens we rescued thought we were being disrespected by being called breeders."

"I remember hearing about that." Turning to our queen I ask curiously, "What term would you use to describe a male used expressly for breeding?"

"We don't have that on Earth. Every male who is physically able tries to get his wife pregnant. There are so few males that everyone is hoping to end up with a baby boy."

I become ever more curious as the conversation rolls along. "If every male is breeding, who cares for the young?"

"What young? Our males have experienced a drop in their sperm count, meaning very few of them can get a woman pregnant. The goal is for couples to have as many children as possible but most are lucky to have one or two. The days of large families including six or seven children are gone on Earth."

"I knew your planet was dying. I didn't realize your people were as well."

Tisha's hand trembles and her metal cup slips to the floor, clattering against the cold metal flooring. Before any of us can respond, Hero is at her side. He squats, slipping an arm around her. "Are you well, my sweet?"

She nods and bends down to retrieve the cup. Thankfully, she'd drank most of the tea so not much is staining the floor. "I was shocked by something Hatch said. I've never really thought about it like that, but I'm sure you're right about our people being in the middle of dying out. It's just shocking to realize that in a few generations there probably won't be any people on Earth."

Hero shoots me an exasperated look for upsetting our queen. Scooting her chair up to the table with her sitting in it, he adjusts her plate. Kane drops another cup of tea on the table and tugs the empty one from her grasp. Jerking over a chair to the corner of the table, Hero slides into it. "Come, let us eat. Save the mourning for your people until another time, for there is nothing you can do to save them."

I gape at Hero, thinking he just made things ten times worse. I'm relieved when our queen perks up. "We'll just see about that."

"If you bid us save the people of Earth, we will be happy to take on the task. However, know this. Your clan is configured to care for a single human queen."

"It just occurred to me that as long as females are leaving Earth and making families, humans will never truly die out."

"I'm certain you are right. I was just trying to communicate that your males are not nearly smart enough to solve complex geopolitical problems of your world, much less figure out why your male genome is failing."

She laughs and chucks the side of one hand up under his chin. "That's a bit of a mouthful. That last sentence ranks right up there with your bountiful breasts comment from last night."

Kane finds her comment funny but Jax and I are lost. Her breasts are bountiful. I have no idea why it is amusing to point that out. Kane clears that up: "Bountiful is a word humans use in association mostly with food. Voluptuous is the term I would use for your breasts."

Our new queen frowns at him as he heaps her plate full of food. "Let's leave my breasts out of this."

Her good mood has returned, so I think that is teasing. Determined to get her attention back on me, I boast, "I have nice breasts for a male, if anyone would like to see."

Jax dips a piece of bread in sauce before speaking. "Don't listen to him. As far as pectorals go, the real contest would be between Hero and Kane. They both have huge muscles."

Though he's not wrong, I refuse to be seen as lesser by our queen. "It is not size but definition that matters."

Hero chews the bit he's stuffed into his face and swallows before joining the conversation about pecs. "Mine are the best in the clade, for I never miss a day of training. However, I suggest that we all present for inspection with bare chests this evening and allow our new queen to decide which among her males has the best pectorals."

Tisha stops in mid bite, with her human-style fork poised in midair. Her face gets that mischievous look again and then she lowers her fork. "I might be up for a little show and tell. I'll warn you all ahead of time that I don't like grabby males. That means you'd better keep your hands to yourself."

I speak before thinking my word choices through. "Any male who touches you without permission will end up with a blood stub."

The entire room goes silent and I realize that perhaps that is not the best image to draw in a queen's mind when she is in the middle of consuming food. Rather than reprimand me, she holds her fist up in the air and grins. "Fist bump. I'm right there with you on that one."

I bring my knuckles up and touch hers, trying to keep my claws retracted so as not to harm her delicate hands.

"You guys are much cooler than I thought when we first met. So, what's on the agenda today?"

"We have staggered our shifts throughout the day so you will always have one of us at your side. Kane wishes you to meet his sire. Jax will show you our medical center and perform a medical exam, since Hero took you straight to our quarters upon arrival. You can spend some time with your queen friend, the Sonarian. When you are finished, Hero wishes to teach you some rudimentary self-defense in our training rooms. I would like to invite you to dine with me for lunch and plan to introduce you to the other human queens aboard this vessel. That is assuming you wish to speak to them."

"I would enjoy meeting them and love to spend some time picking their brains."

Without pausing, I respond lightly, "I do not believe you will be permitted to inspect anyone's brain this day. Such things are not permitted among our people."

She stares at me as if she cannot tell whether or not I am serious. When I grin, she does as well. "I was told Jax was the fun-loving one, yet here you are teasing me like we've known each other for a hundred years."

"If you were a hundred years old, I would still desire to be chosen by you, my beauteous queen."

"Yep, that's me, the beauteous queen with the bountiful breasts."

We laugh, though our plan was to maintain proper decorum for our first meal with Queen Latisha. That she is easy to talk to and accepting of our ways is a blessing. It gives me hope that she might yet choose us.

Also, seeing her interact with Hero warms my heart. Our normally melancholy warrior is smiling and in good spirits. He's so wrapped up in his new queen that I've seen one of his wings touch the ground. That is a breakdown in discipline that I never thought to see in such a proud warrior. To watch him let down his guard this way makes him seem more like family than ever. I smile to myself when his tail comes out to slip around her ankle and she smiles up at him. It is sweet to watch them together. I am likely the only one to see from my angle because we are sitting around the table. "It almost slipped my mind that we promised the peacekeeper that he could meet with you at some point today. He's keen on making sure you are being well treated."

"I'm fine with that. It sounds like our day is shaping up to be a busy one." The lightness in her voice communicates she is fine with our plan but I worry that we may be over-taxing her.

"If you wish to rest today, we can make arrangements for the activities to be rescheduled."

"I don't know if you realize this or not, but I've spent the last three months running around the city, shoveling garbage and sorting recycling. I'm not too weak to walk around your fine ship for the day." Her voice doesn't sound angry but it has a hard edge that I don't like one bit.

The room goes silent as we all envision our lovely queen enduring such hardships. When no one speaks, she does. "Look, I've told all of you a dozen times that I'm no queen. I'm just a woman who barely scratched out a living on Earth, signed up for the galactic brides program to get money for my family and a better life. I'm nothing special, especially after the life I've lived the last three years."

My hand is resting casually on the table. It slowly clenches into a tight fist as I fight the urge to explode at hearing about her impossibly difficult life. "You words stir such anger in me, my queen. I wish the peacekeeper had not executed your captors, for I would like nothing more than to rip them limb from limb." I'm shamed by the emotion in my quivering voice and the fact that I have apparently stunned our new queen into silence.

Kane tries to patch our happy day back together. "Among the Draconians, males who harm a queen are put to death. Obedience to the queens of every species is our sworn duty. To see a queen suffer provokes rage in the deepest recesses of our souls. Please do not think badly of our need to protect, for it is something that has been bred into us for thousands of years."

For once our queen is not smiling. Her face is as serious as mine. "Before I was abducted I would have been shocked by your clan leader's words. Having been enslaved and on the receiving end of the pain and misery dealt by my masters has changed my perspective a bit. My new creed is death to every single being who would dare to harm or enslave an innocent."

Her vicious words settle over us, making me feel more strongly than ever that this queen was meant to be ours. Our new queen understands us more than I ever thought a human female could. She comes slowly to her feet, and without even glancing at each other we move forward, surrounding her. Instead of pushing us away when we need her tenderness, she pulls us closer. We're desperate to protect her and she craves our protection. When her hands land on her protector, she triggers his camouflage. Her hands move from one of us to the next, smoothing over our cheeks and touching our arms in an effort to make sure we are well. Her soft hands landing on our exposed skin affects all of us as strongly as it does Hero. May the gods forgive me, but her fleeting touch feels like being blessed by a true goddess.

When we begin to move back, the spell is broken. Yet we look at each other with new eyes. Knowing that we need to protect our queen solidifies us as a family unit. Believing that she will be there to soothe our battle-weary hearts and bodies is the only assurance I need to risk everything I value for her sake.

Jax and I prepare to leave her in Kane's capable care. For some reason Hero takes her aside and they speak privately before he attaches a com device to the shoulder of her suit. His careful manner may be an indication of how he will protect her moving forward or our clade's protector may be harboring some concerns about leaving her with our breeder. I would not have accepted Kane into our clade if I didn't have the utmost trust in him.

It dawns on me that his mating scent has receded. Cognitively I know that means he is with child. Somehow it does not seem real that a queen with such depth of character is truly mated to our Hero. With any luck we will be chosen as well. I must admit to looking forward to holding their young, for in a clade all hatchlings belong to the clade, rather than the male who sired them.

Hero brushes his lips over hers and we head out the door. Glancing over my shoulder, I watch Kane slip his wing around her. When the door slides shut, I force myself to walk away. She does not need to be overwhelmed by us hovering around her. She needs space to get to each of us. Looking down, I force my feet to start walking.

LATISHA

I'M STILL REELING FROM HATCH GOING A BIT OFF THE rails. I wouldn't have thought these men were so sensitive to women getting hurt, but if what happened just now is any indication, they take that shit very seriously. Talking about my past really triggered an emotional reaction in the overly protective men.

The way they all clustered around me should have felt strange. They needed me to console them and let them know I had not been broken by my savage experiences. One reason I was wary of joining a clade was because I didn't think I could handle all their emotional needs. Things got a little tense there for a minute and I did handle it. Calming them down wasn't even hard. In fact, it felt like the most natural thing in the entire world. I'm not only feeling more confident but I'm starting to actually like them.

Kane's deep voice draws me from my internal musings. "You seem deep in thought, my queen."

Unlike with Hero, I keep a bit of space between me and Kane. His wing is still wrapped around me, but he smells different and his wing isn't as cozy. Maybe I'm wary because of what Hero said about breeders. Looking up into his handsome face, I see nothing that gives me cause to think he's duplicitous. "I'm just thinking about Hatch's clade."

"I have now been accepted into the clade as well."

"Congratulations. I'm sure you'll be a good fit."

"It must feel strange to you being in our clade quarters. You've chosen Hero and the other members of our clade are approaching you, wishing to be selected as well."

I smile because he gets it. "It does feel like I've got one foot in and one foot out of a turbulent situation at the moment."

"You have lovely feet. I'll settle for one being in our clade until we can convince the other to join."

Chuckling, I bump his hip with mine playfully. "You're starting to sound like a guy with a foot fetish."

He gazes down at me with a bit of a grin. "I secretly love the claws that tip each finger on human queens. They are so delicate and non-threatening. Polishing yours would be an honor."

"You polish claws, I mean nails?" I'm totally taken aback. He seems like a rough and tumble warrior.

"I'm a fully trained breeder. I polish claws, give body massages and am well-schooled in how to cater to a queen's every need. I also know how to fight and wield a weapon. That makes me equal parts breeder and warrior."

A deep male voice chides him gently from the doorway. "Queens like humble males not braggarts, my scion."

Kane's head comes up and he grins. "We have arrived at my sire's quarters. I feel certain he has prepared thoroughly to receive a queen this day."

"My scion knows me well. Greetings, Queen Latisha. Welcome to my home."

Kane's father is even larger and more impressive physically than Hero. We follow him into a luxuriously appointed room. It might be about the size of our clan quarters but it's filled with interesting artifacts. Gentle amber lighting gives the room a happy glow and thick animal print rugs cover the floors. "You have a nice home, sire of Kane." I think this is the correct phrasing because a couple of males referred to me as queen of Hero in the dining hall.

The older drone laughs as we take seats on his settee. "If my scion were half as well-trained as he claims, he would have given a proper introduction."

Kane's voice changes, becoming a little harsher. "We do not introduce our queens to other breeders. You know this, my sire."

His father seems more amused than annoyed with his errant son. Leaning forward, he extends one hand for a human-style handshake. "Forgive my jealous son. Only Kane would bring a prospective queen to meet me and be too jealous of his own sire to make proper introductions."

I grin, even though Kane makes a disgruntled sound from beside me.

"I am Roan. Know that you are welcome in my home whenever the need should arise. I welcome you as a daughter."

"That's really sweet. I can almost see why your son might be worried. If I'd met you first, you would be at the top of my list of potential love interests."

The older man laughs, clearing pegging me for a flattering tease. "I do not think you would enjoy tending all the young in my nursery, young queen. A few are still tiny and cute." Cutting his eyes to his simmering son, he adds light-heartedly, "Most of them are at the challenging stage where they have not yet managed to control their baser instincts."

He's referring to Kane's jealousy. I press my lips together to keep from laughing and sneak a glance at Kane. He's barely holding it together. For some reason, I don't find this situation funny anymore. Reaching out to grasp his hand, I speak out of turn. "I certainly hope Kane falls into that category. I look forward to enjoying some of his baser instincts in the coming days."

All the anxiety drains from Kane's face as I give his hand a gentle squeeze. He's momentarily stunned and then a tiny smile curves up the corners of his mouth. "You like me?"

"I sure do. You saved me down on that planet and I'd have to be blind not to notice that you're smokin' hot."

I love the way his facial expression shifts to one of happiness and pride. "It is an honor to serve you, my queen."

"Well, I'm not yours quite yet but I can see us all being a clan in my mind's eye now."

"I am pleased to be considered, by such a bountiful queen."

The hot dragon warrior is making an inside joke and I can't help but laugh. I feel so welcomed by Kane and his father that I dare to ask the question that's been weighing on my mind. "If it's not considered rude, may I ask why warriors are suspicious of breeders?"

Roan's expression shutters in an instant, making me think I've really stepped in the crap with that question. Kane quietly explains, "Our clade's warrior has experienced a queen's claw. I believe he feels betrayed by one of our kind."

Roan stands and walks away. I think for a moment that I might have really offended him but he returns with refreshments on a hovering tray. When it lowers in front of us, I see it's more like a mini banquet of finger foods and an assortment of beverages.

Roan looks over his offerings and choses a small carafe filled with a nearly clear blue liquid. Tipping it into a tiny glass, he begins to speak. "My scion was concerned that you might like of me strongly because I have bred for queens. Before our crew was rescued by the human queens and brought to this dimension things were much different."

I speak up, hoping to save him a bunch of time in his explanation. "Hero told me about how cruel your own queens were and how they liked to play males off against each other, especially warriors and breeders."

"Who is Hero?"

Again Kane explains. "Our new queen did not think Drac's name was dignified so she gifted him with one she thought better suited him."

I cringe because it sounds kind of pompous.

Roan smiles warmly. "I am certain that such a kindness won you his devotion."

I jerk back, stunned by what he's implying. "You make it sound like a calculated ploy to get him to like me."

"Was it not?"

I can't keep the indignation from my voice. "Of course it wasn't. I really care for Hero. He's a nice man."

Smiling, Roan replies, "Then you are not much like our former owners. Draconian queens own the males under their command, much like you own the clothes you wear. Since we were all very aware of the lack of personal power we had, most males did not soften themselves to a female. They were vicious and only a fool would grow a liking for a person who thought of you as a mere possession."

Selecting a drink for himself, Roan sits back in his seat to continue his story. "Breeders had it much worse than warriors, for warriors could go on missions, had duties to attend to and could stay out of their queen's way much of the time. They weren't seen as valuable, so they were rarely targeted by a queen's wrath. We breeders were forever under the claw of a queen from the day we were born. Only death could release us from their chambers. Our queens were forced to play mind games to get any of us to even put up a pretense of cooperation. Many thought it better to die young than feel their claws for a long lifetime. Such were my thoughts upon coming of age."

"I honestly didn't know about how you were treated before coming to this sector. I apologize if my question stirred up bad memories."

Roan sighs and his expression relaxes into a faint smile. "I am continually amazed by how sensitive and polite human queens can be. Do not regret asking questions about things you wish to know out of fear for my wellbeing. I am now a strong male and wish you to fully understand our history. It will give you the wisdom to settle disputes if they arise among your males."

I let that roll around in my head for a moment. There is going to be conflict and I'm the one who's expected to resolve it. I guess that I kind of expected that.

"Before we came here, our former queen had half a dozen breeders. Though I was among them and spawned several times, the one who took the brunt of her abuse was Pern. Draconian queens are damaged by a parasite that feeds on the suffering of others. Therefore they tormented us endlessly. When digging into us with her claws no longer worked, our queen would make us watch as they reaped our young."

A sick feeling churns in my stomach as his words sink in. "What do you mean by reap?"

Tilting his head slightly, the older man breaks it down for me. "Reaping is killing. Our queen reaped any eggs that did not look perfect when we spawned. She came back several times as the eggs were maturing to perform inspections. I remember our queen being increasingly frustrated because none of her breeders had spawned a little queen to one day take her place. Queens are rare and sought after. In her frustration, she would reap the males eggs all the harder."

"I can't even imagine doing something like that."

"All breeders are different. Where Pern was emotionally strong, I was weak. Our queen, Rovanda, reaped Pern's young in his presence. She knew doing such to me would cause my mind to break so she did it behind my back. Between breeding cycles, our queen would not be denied her opportunity to feed on our misery. It was in those days that she tormented us to the point of breaking with her claws. Few beings know this, but there is a point where the pain no longer registers. When that happened, her only recourse was to turn to damaging the ones we loved." Swallowing thickly, he pushes on. "My closest friend was Mathadar, the warrior mated to the queen in charge of this vessel. Most of his many scars are from her abusing him to get to me. Hero is Pern's only living sibling. Rovanda used Hero to get to Pern and it caused him to immediately capitulate to whatever she wanted."

"Hero didn't tell me about any of that."

"Since we were both Rovanda's breeders, Pern and I are close. I know he still feels guilty for the pain she inflicted on his hatch mate. I suspect Hero feels shame that he allowed her to use him in such a despicable manner again Pern. I can assure you that no male had a choice."

"Why didn't you all turn on her? She was one and you were many."

Something dark passes over his face. "It is not done among our people. Queens rule and males submit." Words seem to fail him, so he takes another sip of his drink. I can see his hands are trembling. I feel awful for all the pain they've suffered, both mentally and physically.

Kane also tries to explain what his father cannot. "You must understand that our entire galaxy was ruled by queens. If we were to overthrow one queen, the others would have killed every male on our ship, right down to the hatchlings. There would have been nowhere to hide and no species would have offered us shelter. Our queens were twice the size of even the largest male on our ship. They were bred to be cunning and ruthless. Many systems were set in place to ensure we were never in a position to revolt."

Roan jumps back into the conversation. "That was until the human queens visited our galaxy. They were willing to fight on our behalf and inspired us to fight for ourselves. Queen Cassandra fought face to face with our Draconian queen and just when we thought our cause was lost, Pern stepped into the fight. He killed his own queen with her most deadly weapon and in doing so threw his support behind our human rescuers."

Goosebumps break out across my skin as he finishes his dramatic tale of how they were freed. Finally, Roan adds the missing piece of the puzzle that explains Hero's reluctance to trust breeders even though his brother was one. "I believe the parasites infecting our queens did not keep control of their personalities at all times. There were times when my queen seemed almost normal, particularly after a session of profoundly abusing one of our males." Though Kane makes a noise of disapproval, his father continues. "It was during these moments of sanity that I thought we were making a connection and I wished it to last in hopes it would draw her completely from her madness. I spoke once of Pern's brother and I should have known better."

The reality of their situation dawns on me. "Pern had spent a lifetime protecting that secret and you let the cat out of the bag."

Roan nods, his expression shuttered. "Before discovering that, Rovanda was frustrated by her lack of control over him. He had no apparent weaknesses. Once she discovered Hero, she went overboard teaching Pern that all males were weak before the might of their queens. I had never seen true brutality until that moment and it horrified me that all that suffering was because of me. I quickly realized she was evil from the inside out and no amount of bonding with me or any other male would ever fix that."

Though we talk of other things and Roan's hospitality is flawless, I can't stop thinking about my poor Hero being needlessly tormented by an evil queen twice his size. No wonder he loved being put in the dominant position when we were naked together. I suddenly wonder about a good many things.

When Kane ushers us out of his father's quarters, I wait for the door to close before speaking. "I would like to meet Hero's brother, Pern. Is he on this ship?"

Kane freezes almost in mid step. "I do not think that would be a very good idea, my queen. Pern does not take visitors."

"Show me his door. If he turns me away, I will leave with no hard feelings."

Buttoning his lip, Kane walks me down three doors and waves his hand over the scanning plate beside the door. When the door slides open, a large male is standing in the doorway.

He looks so much like my Hero that my throat closes up. Unlike Hero, his coloring is deep and rich and his wings are smoother and more attractive. However, the same facial feathers and dark eyes study me for a brief moment. "Greetings, Queen Latisha. I have been expecting a visit from you."

"Greetings, Pern. May I come in?"

Stepping back, I realize he has something tucked into the crook of his arm. It's got wings and claws like his own but it's definitely not a child of their kind. It has fur and big yellow eyes. I step past the two of them and he hits the button to close his door before Kane steps through.

Shock rips through me. "That was a little rude. We could have just asked him to wait outside."

The man's blank expression seems to be plastered over a melancholy one. "Among our people, simply closing the door is considered more polite than asking a visitor not to enter. It saves an otherwise awkward conversation between the two males."

That makes a semblance of sense. I follow him over to a tiny seating area. His chambers are richly appointed but much smaller than Roan's quarters. I remember Roan has young but none of Pern's survived. My heart aches for Hero's abused brother.

His eyes are curious and I begin to wish I had taken more care with my appearance. He's used to royalty and I've got my hair slung over one shoulder in a careless braid. He speaks almost immediately. "I am pleased Hero took a queen who was kind enough to gift him with a proper name."

I'm still emotional from hearing about all their abuse so I stammer a dumb answer. "I didn't really mean to rename him. He told me about males who aren't special being named Drac and it kind of made me angry. Your brother really is my hero, so the name seemed appropriate. I honestly think he's really special and unique."

He relaxes, dropping the pet into his lap. "Human queens are easy to talk to." His expression is still kind of blank, and for the life of me, I feel as though I'm missing something important.

"Yeah, we're a pretty docile bunch compared to what you're used to." Okay, I'm just saying one dumb thing after another. Pulling my scattered thoughts together, I try to speak as to why I've come. "I want you to know that I really care about your brother and I'd never do anything to hurt him or you."

"I never for a moment thought you would. Human females seem kind and generous according to all that I know of them."

"Yet you don't have one."

Finally, a ghost of a smile crosses his lips. "You are observant. I have had my fill of queens. Being left with no young of my own, I will wait and spoil my brother's little scion. I have been excited about this since he told me about being chosen."

I can't help but grin. "I can't wait for us to have little ones. I hope they have Hero's camouflaging abilities. That's a really cool and useful trait to have."

His eyebrows rise. "You find value in the quality that marks us both as being among the most primitive of our kind. It is a trait I learned to hide early on to avoid punishment."

Leaning over, I lower my voice. "Want to know a secret?" After he nods, I continue. "When Hero and I cuddle, his camouflage shifts to match my skin. It's the most amazing thing I've ever seen and it makes me feel like he was made just for me."

Sitting his pet aside, the reticent man scoots forward with his wings relaxing behind him. He takes my hands in his, but before he can speak, the door slides open and Hero comes stalking into the room. Rather than letting my hands go, Pern grips them tighter. "Greetings, spawn mate."

Hero slides to a stop and I watch the door close behind him. Kane is still on the other side with his arms folded in front of him. Hero looks a little panicked. Looking at me, he speaks, "If I had known you wished to visit my kin, I would have brought you myself." Shifting his gaze to Pern, he asks cautiously, "Are you now accepting visitors, my hatch mate? If this is not a good day for you, we can postpone our visit for another time."

"All is well. I was just about to tell your lovely new queen that she is welcome to visit me anytime. From now on, if I answer the door, I am well."

Relaxing a bit, Hero strolls over and sits beside me on the settee. "I did not think you would be so open to coming face-to-face with another queen, even a human one."

Allowing my hand to slip from his, Pern's expression shuts down again. "I have no use for queens. Though you do not believe me, I do enjoy my solitary life. My wish has always been for you to find happiness. If you have found it in this human queen, then I am grateful for it."

Hero's hand drifts down to scratch at his hip. His brother's expression morphs into an annoyed one. "Do not scratch." Hero's hand flies back so fast I can barely see it move.

I hate to think he's got something wrong and isn't getting it looked at. "Do you need to see a healer? If you have a skin problem they can probably give you a topical ointment or something."

Pern's expression morphs into one of amusement. "I agree with your queen, hatch mate. Go and let the healer examine your skin."

"Is brother and hatch mate the same thing?"

Pern responds almost chipperly. "Hatch mates are siblings from the same spawning. Males can spawn many times during their lifetimes. Each spawning can result in multiple hatchlings."

"How many?"

Shooting Hero a quick glance, he speaks carefully. "Warriors can spawn anywhere from one to four eggs. Assuming they all survive, it would result in between four to eight young. Most eggs contain only one child but some contain two. Hero and I were hatched from a spawning of twenty-three because our father was a queen maker. Neither of us was lucky enough to inherit the queen making gene. As a breeder I can spawn up to a dozen young at a time but queen makers spawn more frequently and in larger numbers."

"I'm glad Hero is not one of them. We'll be running ourselves ragged taking care of up to eight. God, I hope it's just two or three. I don't want our little ones to feel like they're missing out on our attention because there are so many." I can now clearly see the reason Hero thinks we need a clan. It makes sense.

Hero smiles down at me but his brother's deep rich laugh catches me by surprise. "Shall I tell her, hatch mate, or will you?"

"When Draconian males mate with a queen, their mating scent does not stop perfuming the air until the male is with child."

"Well you were smelling absolutely divine there for a minute." Catching myself before I can misstep, I quickly add, "Not that you don't smell nice now. I promise you smell fantastic."

"Your new queen is quite adorable. What my hatch mate is attempting to communicate is that he is even now spawning for you, Queen Latisha. His mating scent has retreated and one of the very first symptoms is skin irritation. The sack in his hip where the eggs will grow fills with fluid. I have often heard that for some it can itch."

I'm almost too stunned to speak. Hero looks a little unsure. "You're carrying our child?"

He nods. "If it pleases you."

"Well, I'm all kinds of pleased to have a hot Draconian husband and a child all at the same time. Can I see the spot?"

Standing, Hero peels back his uniform top and pulls it down. Pern leans over, running his finger over a hand-sized swell that's barely noticeable. "That can be nothing else. You are definitely carrying."

I grab his hand and begin pulling him up. "We should go see the healers and let them have a look."

Pern laughs. "You must wait at least ten cycles for the healers to have anything to look at except itchy skin."

That takes the steam out of my idea real quick and I stop pulling on him. He slips one wing around me and tugs me to his side. "You are late for your meeting with Jax. Come, I will escort you. You can talk to him about spawning all you wish."

I step out and give Pern a quick hug before pulling back and looking up at him. His tiny pet is jumping between our legs, tripping over our feet. "Thanks for talking with me today. I hope we get to visit a lot. I want to hear all about what your brother was like as a child."

"You should visit only when you have a long time to stay, for I have many such stories."

"Maybe we can do lunch every day and you tell me one. That way we can string out the fun for a long time."

Holding my shoulders in his hands his expression is bright. "I would like that very much, Queen Latisha."

"You can call me Tisha."

"I would be honored to call you by your preferred name, Queen Tisha."

Oh boy, these guys just do not get it. They don't seem to be able to let go of the queen title for every woman. I guess it's not so bad. I'm getting used to it already.

When the door opens my entire clan is standing around nervously. Hero announces quietly, "My hatch mate was having a good day today."

Everyone relaxes and it makes me wonder what the poor man is like when he's not having a good day.

I cannot imagine what made Kane decide to take our new queen for an impromptu visit with Pern of all people. I love Hero like a brother, but his brother is seriously unwell. I am relieved that today he was functional but other days he screams and claws at his skin over the young our former queen reaped. Other days he sinks into a deep depression over killing the evil bitch. Though my soul aches for his losses, Pern is not someone to leave an innocent queen alone with.

Shooting him a withering look, I step out and take his place at her side. No one knows quite what to say, so I speak up. "I'm pleased you enjoyed your visits with Roan and Pern. Would you like to see where I work?"

She steps under my outstretched wing and we begin moving towards the medical unit. I can hear the rest of my clan quietly arguing the moment we are almost out of hearing distance. To cover their voices I make polite conversation. "I checked on your Solarian friend. She is much improved and looking forward to a visit from you."

"Did you know Hero is carrying?"

"I assumed he was, since his mating scent is not as potent. How do you feel about that?"

"I actually have a million questions."

We get on vertical transport to level three, where the medical unit is.

"Don't tell me you don't know how babies are made, Queen Tisha." My gentle teasing is well received. I like making her laugh and decide it is my new life's ambition.

"I thought I knew all about that, but where I come from males do not carry young."

"Draconian males require only contact with the pheromones of a compatible female to activate our reproductive systems. It used to happen often for the males standing guard for our former queen when she engaged with her breeders."

"I don't understand."

"Our species was engineered. Our DNA was spliced with that of dragons and then tinkered with by mixing in genetic material from other sentient species. It happened thousands of years ago and it is unclear why this was done."

"I heard something about that when I was still on Earth. We had legends of dragons but always thought they were mythical creatures."

"Perhaps your early ancestors came into contact with a species who kept them. They are not native to our galaxy but they apparently transplanted well because they are prolific on many planets in the modern age."

"I'd love to see one in real life someday." She looks up at me nervously and amends her statement. "I'd like to see them from a safe distance I mean."

"I would like that as well. I have had the pleasure of visiting few planets and none have had dragons."

"Humans like to make lists of things to do before they die. I'm adding seeing a real live dragon to mine."

"I would much like to see this list of yours one day, my queen, so I might ascertain if our interests are similar."

"If we're playing show and tell, you'll have to show me yours first."

I can't help but attempt the human flirtation. "Are we still talking about lists, because I have more entertaining things to show you than my list of interests. I am still interested in learning all your secrets though, make no mistake about that."

The last bit of darkness lifts from her face as she replies. "If you end up doing my physical, you'll be able to have a little peek inside and there's no telling what you might find."

"If only a queen's secrets could be so easily learned, my pretty queen."

"I really like your whole clan. You're good people."

I'm taken aback, unsure what won me such a nice compliment. "We are honored and most eager for the revealing ceremony tonight. We've been speculating about whether the males are the only ones who will bare their chests or if you will choose to gift us with a glimpse of your form as well."

Her mouth falls open just as we reach the medical unit. It takes her a moment to remember that we arranged the baring of chests to see who has the most pectoral definition. Grinning, she shrugs. "I might bare some skin but that no grabbing rule is still in effect."

My feet come to a stop and I turn to her. "I would never touch a queen without permission, nor would any of my clan."

She stares at me for a long hard moment before speaking. "You know something? I honestly don't think any of you would. Maybe I need to get my anxiety about that under control."

"If you trust nothing else aboard this vessel, trust in our wish to protect you from all danger, even danger from within." We walk into my healing pod and I begin prepping the equipment for a deep scan.

"Don't tell me you have trust issues with breeders too?"

Turning to look at her over my shoulder, I try to figure out what she means. It takes a moment to remember that Hero has trouble because of his past. Rather than get into my friend's personal challenges, I simply state my stance on that issue. "I have no problems trusting breeders and especially none trusting Kane. Rest assured, you are safe with our clade."

"I'm glad. Sorry if I'm being nosey."

"I don't know what that means but we can begin the scan with your nose if you like. Step onto the scanning platform and I'll get this over with quickly so you can visit with your friend."

"That's just a saying. You can start the scan anywhere you like." She steps on the slightly elevated platform and I begin the scan. I see several things that concern me, not the least of which is a tear in her abdominal wall. The human healers call it a hernia and must operate to fix it. I will simply give her a small injection of nanobots programed to repair the damage. I program a small dose of bots and continue the scan. She has a misaligned disk and lower than normal levels of three critical nutrients. I program two more doses of bots and load them in three hypo-sprays.

"You have several minor issues. I can fix them all with three shots. Most queens want to know what physical problems they have prior to initiating the procedures to correct them. Is this your wish as well?"

"Who wouldn't want to know their own medical problems?"

She sounds angry with my phrasing. I immediately attempt to remediate that problem. "Believe it or not, our warriors become irritated if we attempt to explain the medical issue our scanners reveal. They just want to be treated and released so they can go back to training or battle and get more injuries. It's a never-ending cycle, a frustrating one for healers."

Her frown clears and she rolls her eyes. "I'm with you. If something's wrong with my body, I want to know what it is."

Tickled by her interest in medicine, I go over what I found and she consents to my treatments. When I am finished she stretches her arms over her head and it brings her bountiful breasts up, making them more noticeable. I try not to stare and am rewarded with a warm hug. "Thanks for taking care of my health. I haven't felt this good in a long time."

"I am pleased to care for all your medical needs. The only time I would involve another healer would be if you required specialized treatment that I did not feel confident to provide."

"Well, on Earth doctors aren't allowed to treat their own family members. The general opinion is they are too close to the situation to be objective."

Shock rips through my chest, leaving a raw ache. "Draconians are just the opposite. If there is a healer in a family he would treat all his own family, thinking no other could possibly be as diligent about their care."

"Our clan is lucky to have you. I like that you're more

human-sized. That means we can spar and play physical games the others would never consider because they'd be afraid of hurting me."

"My size is generally thought to be a disadvantage among our people. I was chosen to be a healer because my family advocated strongly against me being reaped due to being smaller."

She steps forward again and wraps her arms around my torso.

"I like human hugs but I am unclear why I am getting them. If I understood more, I could have some control and perhaps get more of them."

She pulls back with a smile. "I do that sometimes when I'm thankful or have strong feelings. Your first hug was for healing me and the second was my panicked reaction to thinking about how close you came to not existing."

"I know my sire fought for me and in the end our queen didn't care enough about the goings on with simple warriors to care. I'm lucky my sire wasn't a breeder. I'd have been reaped for sure."

"I'm really glad you made it. You're an amazing person. If we end up making babies, we've not allowing any of them to get hurt."

I slip my wing around her back and reply honestly. "Our young will probably get hurt at some point. They are born with wings and become mobile pretty fast. It's inevitable that they will get small injuries and maybe a few serious injuries. I'll do my best to keep everyone healthy."

"We're on the same page there."

A deep voice comes from the doorway. "You didn't bring the female to me as agreed."

Before the peacekeeper can get to my queen, I whirl around and stand protectively in front of her. Though I am small, I will not allow him to take our queen. My hand goes out to rest instinctively on the weapon at my hip. "You do not have permission to visit unannounced. You know this, Crovan. Queen Daisy was very clear on that point."

"I wish to protect my charge."

My queen's hand comes out to stay the hand on my weapon. "I'll talk to him if it saves an argument." I move over slightly and allow her to move forward. An alarm sounds and the lights in the room begin flashing. I move quickly to get in front of her. "What have you done, Crovan?"

"You should not have forbidden me access to my charge. Give her to me, or I will take her."

"My answer is no. You will have to kill me to take her."

"If you keep delaying, neither of us will be around to protect her."

"The alert isn't for you, is it?"

"Clearly you are not the smartest member of your clade. I am but one being and have been divested of my weapons, so I am not the threat your crew is now facing."

I clip my com to my ear and it fills with many warriors giving report. Our engines have failed and we are being boarded. "Hatch is leading a team of fighters to protect the hatchery. When the Moltan have attacked before, they came for our little ones. He is commanding all of us to meet him there. If we get there immediately it will be the safest location in the ship. He's putting three layers of warriors around the hatchery."

I open our emergency cabinet and toss the peacekeeper a weapon. He is at my side immediately, loading his body with weapons. I clip my personal shield to Queen Tisha's uniform and I doubt she even knows what it is. I shove a laser pistol into her hand and activate the shield. I load up with what weapons I can carry and lead the way. Crovan brings up the rear, ensuring none hit us from behind.

Fury spikes in my gut that these beasts always come for our young. The last time, they took Queen Daisy along with some of our unhatched young. The Moltan wish to create a genetically compatible host body for the same parasite that infected our Draconian queens for the last several thousand years. We will fight to the last warrior to keep them from getting a foothold in this sector of space.

Just when Jax and I were starting to bond, the alert sounded. I feel like I'm never going to catch a break. While we hustle to the hatchery, Jax fills us in on the situation. I shiver to think of the parasites infecting women in this sector of space and replicating the mass killing they did where Jax came from. He calls his sector Exion space. I've never heard of it but then again all my time in space was spent in a cage.

A tight glob of red-hot sludge shoots past my arm, melting my uniform. Jax shouts, "They're using plasma weapons, stay back. Be careful not to step where it lands."

Meanwhile, both he and Crovan rush in front of me and the sound of their combined weapons is deafening. Instead of taking out my laser pistol and shooting like a normal person, my hands fly to my ears and I drop to my knees. Something roars like a wounded beast. The deep mournful sound is like nothing I've ever heard. It reminds me of a death keen. My eyes land on the glob of plasma. It's slowly eating through the flooring.

Strong hands land on my upper arms and I am pulled

up to my feet by Jax. He's sweating and has some kind of weapons discharge covering one shoulder of his uniform. And his wings are spread out like the frail covering could protect us from weapons fire. "Are you well, my queen? Can you walk?"

Nodding ridiculously fast, I sputter, "Yes. I'm fine, just a little freaked out."

"Stay at my back. No harm will come to you."

The peacemaker suddenly appears right next to us. He is also covered in some kind of discharge. It's more noticeable against his milky white skin because he doesn't wear clothing. "Not time to talk. We must move. Now."

He takes the lead and Jax frowns, falling into the rear position. Clearly this is also not the time to argue about who gets the lead position. Jax's hands come back out to guide me around our fallen enemies. There are two of them and they're huge. Each has hooves for feet and a large intricate crown of horns in a generous halo above their heads. They're similar to deer antlers but larger, circular and woven together. I've never seen anything like them and am amazed that Jax and Crovan managed to kill them both, especially since they're wearing body armor.

When we near the hatchery Hero runs to my side. My large warrior is normally quiet when he walks but today his feet pound the floor noisily in his haste to get to my side. "Good work, Jax. You protected our queen."

Jax gestures behind us. "I had help."

Hero's eyes meet those of the peacekeeper and he nods at the well-armed man. "Come, we have no time to spare. Hatch is forming the first line of defense. Kane will hold the second line. I will hold the final line here in the hatchery. The more experienced warriors will battle the intruders every step of the way from the loading bay to the first line and then disperse among the battle lines."

Crovan's voice sounds off. "It is a good plan. We must get your queen behind the line, for my future happiness relies upon her survival."

I let the cryptic statement fly by unaddressed. Now is not the time to satisfy my idle curiosity. Jax grabs my hand and pulls me toward a room in the back of this grouping of men. Crovan stays to help hold the line. When we pass through the door, I see we are in some kind of Draconian play area. It's a huge open space and reminds me of a loading bay but there is cute kid-sized exercise or play-ground equipment set up. I also see adorable little alien toys scattered around as if just dropped when they ran. As Hatch works on opening the door, I stoop to pick up a tiny doll. Only it's not really a doll, because it has a snout and fur. I realize it might be their version of a stuffed animal.

I swallow thickly. Jax already told me that they would have put Trovena and her little ones in stasis and hidden her away in one of the large wall units. A healer will stay to monitor them and anyone else who wasn't stable enough to move. I worry for her and her newly born babes. My throat chokes up at the thought of anything happening to them. Jax's harsh voice rises. "Tisha, you must not become detached. We need to stay alert."

Looking up, I realize he's unlocked the door and has been calling me. Taking the toy with me, I step over the threshold and look around while he goes through the complicated process of locking the door again. He's using some kind of encryption process that requires a string of alphanumeric code and a retina scan.

The room is filled with about two dozen children ranging in age from babies to tweens. They stop and stare at me. A little girl who appears to be about five is being held by one of the older males. The term older is being used loosely. The only men in this room are the ones who are clearly too old to fight. The girl has clearly been crying and points to the toy in my hand. I move closer and put the toy in her hand. She clutches it to her chest and her wings flap with happiness.

The older man murmurs quietly, "Thank you. I am Mur and this little gem is Silvia."

I respond in a low tone. "I'm Tisha of the House of Citron. My clade leader sent me here to wait out the battle."

We both look over at Jax. He's finished with the door but stands with one hand pressed against it and the other resting on his chest. Mur whispers, "He feels as though he should be fighting with his clade. They are in danger and he is safe. Even I feel the pull to fight for our queens."

"Well, we need you both here protecting the little ones. If we are to have a future, they must survive."

"The last time the Moltan attacked, we did not know they would be targeting the hatchery so it was not as well protected as it is this day."

"Today, they're not getting any of our hatchlings. My clade will see to that." I hate that Hero is facing enemies in battle when he is carrying our young. But one thing I know about life is it doesn't always give you choices. Sometimes, you just have to make the best of a bad situation.

I walk up to Jax and slip my arms around his waist from behind. Leaning my cheek on the tight knot of his wing, my arms tighten. "I'm worried about them too but I need you here with me, Jax."

He turns and I loosen my arms. His wings come out around both of us, creating a private space for us to whisper. His lips come down on my forehead and he murmurs, "I normally do not worry when we are fighting side by side. Today we're all separated, forcing the enemy to fight though our lines to get to you. I will be your protector of last resort when by all rights it should have been Hero."

"I don't care which clan member is at my side when danger knocks."

He jerks back and stares down at me with questioning eyes.

I nod, trying to take his mind off the battle raging outside. We have no control over that and all the little ones are already being taken care of by the elder males. Rubbing my hands on his chest, I whisper, "I've decided that I don't want to be without any of you. Each of you brings something different to the table and it would be really difficult to even choose which one of you I like the best."

His expression morphs into one of reserved joy, for he is still worried about our loved ones fighting outside this room. "I believe queens like best whichever male's wing they are sheltering under."

"You might be right about that, cause I'm liking you pretty hard right now."

"I was wary about accepting you into our clan in the beginning. Few human women want clans and I knew you would be sought after."

"You do seem a little less impressed with my womanly charms than the others."

"I am impressed with everything about you and find you quite charming." Looking uncomfortable, he finally comes out with it. "I had no wish to tie myself to a queen who could not find love in her heart for us as males."

Cupping his handsome face in my hands, I become aware that his tail is trapped outside the cup of his wings and is beating softly against our legs. "I honestly do care about you. At first I couldn't imagine being with a clan because I thought you would all be fighting over me. I didn't want to see everyone upset all the time and know that I'm the reason for it."

His hands come up to cover mine. "I look forward to seeing you bestowing your affections upon my clade members. They are honorable males and deserve all the love that you see fit to give them."

"I can't wait to see the backside of this battle. When we're all safe and sound in our clan quarters, I'll finally feel like this is over."

"My clade will be ecstatic to know that you have selected us for your human clan. Hero told us that you wished to start a clan of your own."

"I still want us to be called Citron. I love that name."

Jax's face lights up. "Hatch will be thrilled to learn that you plan to keep our clade name. As for myself, I am just happy to have you as our queen."

The entire ship suddenly shakes, causing me to fall onto Jax. His wings snap back so we can catch our balance. Some of the little ones begin crying and the older ones immediately go to their sides. Jax and I mix and mingle, helping out where we can. Neither of us say what we're thinking. That jolt felt like a direct hit to the ship. If that's the case, the battle can't be going well.

## Hatch

I stand shouting orders at the group of fighting warriors. Though I am a new commander, the older commanders obey my orders because they have failed in their duty to hold the enemy off and now must join my ranks to continue the battle. My unit swells from twenty to roughly fifty fighters, with more flowing in from other lost battles.

I'm aware that the battle is being fought on several fronts. One is here, around the hatchery. Another is around the bridge because we can't let them get control of the ship. The final battle is around Queen Daisy's quarters. Though all the other queens are sheltered there, the Moltan want the queen they stole before. Though the reason they fight so hard to get Queen Daisy back is not clear, I know that Darnok will never allow them to touch a hair on her precious head.

Nor will I allow them to get their filthy hands on my own queen. I blast a hole in the horde of enemies clogging the corridor leading to our position. I'm careful to use a particle weapon designed to eat through flesh and leave anything non-biological intact. Unlike our enemy who are using plasma weapons, I have no wish to breach the hull of this vessel. It would suck us all out into space, leaving no one alive to continue the battle.

My blast slows them down for a brief moment. Our warriors surge forward, continuing to pick off the ones trying to scramble back to a secondary position. I toss the particle weapon aside. We only had one charge for the weapon, therefore it is spent.

The peacekeeper is waving around a tiny mechanical device he retrieved from his belt. "There is a swarm about to force their way down the corridor. We'll be overwhelmed. We must fall back."

I yell, "Stand your ground. They must not reach the hatchery." Turning slightly, I open a com channel. "All available warriors converge on my coordinates. Kane, pull your line forward. We need everyone with a weapon here immediately. Hero, stand firm where you are. You are our last line of defense. If all is lost, take our queen and the little ones to safety in the primary escape pod."

As I raise my weapon to join the fight once more, I hear the others sounding off their acknowledgement and acceptance of my orders. Normally, pride would surge in my chest that all are following my orders without complaint. However, it is all I can do to keep the terror at bay. If we lose this battle our precious queen will be taken. The thought of Latisha being tormented with endless medical tests as the Moltan attempt to create a perfect host for their parasite propels me to ever bolder action.

The peacekeeper has a weapon in each hand and is taking out more of the enemy than I am. Does that make him a better protector than me? Suddenly, all that matters is killing more of the enemy than the male who rescued my queen. I'm vaguely aware that this is not something to feel competitive about, yet I do. My way of fighting is much different than his. I back up against the wall, pull up my battle rifle and begin aiming for their faces. I take a deep breath and pull the trigger over and over again. I don't even take the time to watch them fall. If they survive a shot to the head, the other warriors can claim the kill. I'm going for sheer numbers.

The moment my laser rifle loses its charge, Kane is there pressing another to my hand before dropping down to begin taking out our enemy with a similar rifle. His is meant for sniping and he's taking out the ones all the way in the back as we work on the ones surging forward. Though we aren't even coming close to killing them all, my confidence grows. Between Crovan, Kane and myself, we are shearing down the numbers dramatically. I don't have time to check but I'm hoping our losses are minimal.

The battle rages for what seems like forever. We eventually press our advantage, forcing them back through the corridor and back across the ship. I'm careful to make sure we are clearing each area and sealing it off as we go. The sheer number of locked sections they would need to navigate virtually ensures the ones we protect will be able to make a safe escape should the tide of battle turn.

At one point Darnok and his team meet up with us. As always Roan is at his side. Pern is fighting this day as well. Roan reaches out to clasp his scion's shoulder. Kane excitedly tells him about our success. "We turned the battle and have only to force them the rest of the way from the ship."

Pern asks grimly, "Where is my brother?"

I jerk my chin in the direction of the hatchery. "He and his team are holding as the last line of protection for our hatchlings. Our queen and Jax are there as well."

His chest relaxes. Rather than stay or talk with us, he wanders off in the direction of the battle.

"We should all follow Pern's good example."

Kane agrees with me. "Yes. I will not be satisfied until the ship is clear of the enemy and their fallen dead."

There are so many warriors gathered for the final push and with Darnok in charge it can barely be called a battle. Within the hour we have not only pushed them back through the docking ring they entered our ship through, but once their ship detaches Darnok orders our bridge crew to throw everything they have at it. A gigantic explosion rocks our ship although we waited until we were at a safe distance. It makes me wonder what kind of power source the Moltan use to fire their ship's engines.

We quickly begin searching for our wounded and begin transporting them to medical. Soon the medical bays will be filled with our wounded. I com Jax to check on him and our queen.

Jax reports, "We are well. Did the ship get hit? We felt the impact."

"We have finished the battle and are now clearing away the fallen and cleaning away the blood and gore."

"Glad I'm a healer, rather than a member assigned to the clean-up crew. I assume you are calling to let me know to get my ass to the medical unit."

Smothering a smile, I respond, "You would be correct about that, Jax. Your services are urgently needed to assist in treating our wounded."

Hero is also on the line and I give him orders as well. "I want your team to remain in place and keep the hatchery on lockdown, at least until we can clean up the blood and give the ship a final sweep.

"I'll have them stand down but remain in place. Missing a glorious battle is making them irritable, so the sooner you can get us out of here, the better. Jax is needed in the medical unit. Perhaps you and your team can entertain our queen. That should improve their mood."

I can almost hear the growl in Hero's voice. "Yes, but having other males looking at my queen will not improve my mood."

I close off the line before I say something flippant. My battle lust is raging and I don't trust myself not to provoke him further. I begin helping search for wounded. When all my Draconian brethren are in medical, I will help with cleanup and then perhaps visit with our queen.

I stretch my wings and take a deep breath. This day has been filled with all the thing a warrior loves: beautiful queens, a glorious battle and fighting side by side with my brethren. What more could a male ask for in life?

\

When Jax left, I got to spend some time with Hero and his team. Though his team was on their best manners, my Hero was on edge the whole time. They asked dozens of questions about Earth. That didn't surprise me, cause that is our destination. They were also curious about human women.

When we were finally given permission to leave, Hero scooped me up and took me directly to our quarters. When the door shuts behind us he finally seems to calm down a bit. I motion him over to sit with me. "Come and cuddle with me, babe. You look like you're about to crawl out of your skin."

He huffs an exasperated breath and is on the settee beside me so fast I almost don't see him move. The moment my hands begin smoothing down his chest, he relaxes and his camouflage shifts to match my coloring. "I don't like the other warriors having their eyes on what is mine."

Caressing the side of his face, I feel his tail curling up in my lap. "I don't belong to you. I've decided to accept your whole clan, so you're going to have to get used to other men looking at me."

Suddenly, he is all smiles and leans into my touch. "My clade is permitted to look."

I smile up at him. "Be reasonable, Hero. You can't stop people from looking at other people."

"Jax says because I am carrying our young, it makes me more possessive. I wish to rip out the eyes of any males who dare to stare at you with longing."

Realizing that we're getting tangled up in some seriously circular reasoning, I pull him down for a kiss. If I keep his mouth busy, he can't keep complaining about stupid stuff, right? My brain is all on board, all except that piece that's saying I should be helping set the ship back to rights after the attack. Yeah, I totally ignore that part and just keep right on kissing, cause my Hero needs me right now.

We cuddle and I tell him about all the cute little ones I saw. He brings his hand to his side and I'm curious to see the area again. I think maybe asking to see it every five minutes is rude, though, so I don't. When I get pregnant, I wouldn't want my guys lifting my shirt off and on all the time to look at my slowly growing baby bump after all. Hero gets us a couple of cold drinks from the clade's cooling unit and before long the door chimes.

When Hero answers it, Pern is standing there. He's changed out of his armored flight suit and into a normal uniform. Hero grabs his shoulder and pulls him into a hug. They walk into the seating area. "The battle must have been fierce if Darnok brought you out to fight."

"Breeders are not fighters but I did my share this day to see victory to our queens. I came to see that you were both well and to bring you a mating gift." It's then that I notice he has a small container in his hands.

Hero beams at his brother. "That is very thoughtful of you, especially when everyone else was only thinking about our recent battle."

"I care not for fighting. You know this, Hero. It is strange to see you wearing your queen's coloring. It suits you, I think."

I glance down at our joined hands. Bringing his hand to my lips, I murmur, "I have to agree. Why don't you get your brother a drink? Are you hungry after your long battle?"

Pern relaxes back into his seat. "I would take a cold drink if you have one. Food does not sound like a bad idea either."

I nod to Hero who immediately gets on his com as he rises to fetch the drink.

I scoot forward in my seat and give Pern the good news. "I decided to accept the whole clan. Do you think I'm making a good decision?"

I get one of his rare smiles. "You most certainly are, Queen Tisha. The House of Citron will never fail you and give you many wonderful children." He reaches out his hand and offers me the black container. I take it from his hand, realizing it's weightier than I would have imagined.

Setting it in my lap, I try to figure out how to open it. Hero slips a drink into his brother's hand and presses a barely perceptible circle in the center of the top. The lid flips back and tucked neatly inside are jewels. I gasp my surprise. "They're beautiful, Pern."

Hero explains, "They have been in our family for many generations. The rule of Draconian queens has been inconsistent. The younger the queen, the more open and affectionate she can be. Several in our line wore these jewels."

"None for three generations, I'm told." Pern's words are like ice cold water being thrown over us.

I lift out the tray holding what appears to be a masterfully detailed necklace only to find yet more jewels in another tray. I suspect the box is layered with them. "Are you certain you want me to have them? Wouldn't you like to keep some for your own queen? You're still young and surely one day you might find a compatible woman."

Pern's expression shutters and his voice turns cold. "I killed my own queen. Shot her with her own weapon."

He's beginning to get really agitated, so I reach out and grab one of his hands in mine. I squeeze hard enough to get his attention. "You saved your queen by killing the parasite."

For a moment his eyes go wide and then he blinks. After a few moments of thoughtful consideration, he takes a breath. "I never thought of it that way." His eyes become glassy and he swallows thickly. "You are correct, of course you are. I am lucky to finally get the perspective of a queen."

Nodding, I state solemnly, "Promise me something, Pern."

"Anything, Queen Tisha." His expression and tone are as serious as mine.

"If ever one of the symbionts infects me and it can't be removed. Do me a gigantic favor and give me the same mercy you gave your queen. I don't want to end up trapped in my own body watching while the symbiont destroys everything I hold dear."

Hero makes a sound of disapproval but his brother perks up as if my request has given his life new meaning. "I will let nothing stand in my way. If you cannot be saved then you will get a merciful death at my loving hands."

Clutching the box to my stomach, I lean over and give him a long hug. We understand each other. He did nothing wrong and I don't have to worry about the endless misery of being held hostage in my own body. It's a win-win.

Pulling back, all the anxiety and sadness seems to have evaporated. Looking up at Pern, I slide onto my knees and turn to spread out all the jewels on the settee where I was sitting. Hero scoots over to make room. Turning to look over my shoulder, I tell Pern, "I've decided to keep half. If you don't end up with a shiny new wife you can always gift them to me later."

He tosses me an indulgent smile. "Whatever pleases you, sweet queen."

"Come and help me decide which ones look best against my skin."

He happily moves forward and sits back on his haunches. Hero watches us talk and tease each other as we pick through all the jewels. When it's all decided, we pack up the second half and put them back in his cleverly designed box.

I end up wearing one with a round flat yellow stone. It's nice enough to motivate me to pick though the beautiful gowns my clade have stored in our sleeping room. I excuse myself to give Hero and his brother a moment to talk privately. I don't know that giving them time together is necessary but something tells me they have much to discuss.

I take my time, grab a shower and pick out a nice outfit. I should probably feel a bit greedy but I honestly think Pern's nice gift should be displayed to its best advantage. This is also our first evening as a clan. Standing in front of a reflective surface I've thought of as the mirror, I use several of the pins in the drawer of hair grooming supplies my clan gathered to do a really simple updo.

Since I'm kind of quick about my business, I sit on the bed wondering what to do with myself. I guess I could peek out and see if they look like they're engrossed in a private conversation. Doing so, I see that they are seated across from each other and appear to be playing a three-dimensional strategy game of some sort.

Relieved, I slip out and catch Hero's notice first. He almost drops the drink he's holding in an effort to get to his feet. Pern turns around and his expression morphs into one of surprise. It is Pern who actually speaks first. "Do you have a team of breeders hiding in your dressing room or did you actually do all that yourself?"

I can't help but laugh at his hastily spoken words. "I've been told that I clean up real good."

"I should say so. I honestly think you may be the most beautiful queen I have ever set eyes upon."

Teasing him right back, I waltz up to my protector. "If that's true, you really should get out more. I'm nowhere near pretty, much less beautiful."

Hero, who is still looking awestruck, finally remembers how to make words. "You lie, my bountiful queen, for I have never seen your like."

Reaching up to cup his face, I murmur softly, "Aren't you the most attentive male ever to compliment his woman? This is just the reaction I always dreamed of getting when I got myself all fancied up."

He clears his throat. "Stop looking at my queen, Pern."

I pull him down for a light kiss. "Don't start that again. I made myself pretty specifically to be looked at." Hero's not buying that for a minute and he's right not to. I did it to feel good about myself. It's been a long time since I've felt pretty and I like it.

Kane comes barreling through the door and stops short at the sight he sees. The man looks like he's been through the wringer. His uniform is torn and he's got bruises and scratches on his face. His eyes catch mine and he immediately lowers his head. "Apologies, my queen, I did not know you were being intimate with your chosen one."

Pern makes his excuses and heads for the door, barely acknowledging Kane. They may think it's because Kane's a breeder. I suspect it's because he reminds the troubled man of all his young that did not survive.

HERO IS THE ONE WHO FINALLY SPEAKS. "COME AND look your fill of our beautiful new queen, for she has accepted our entire clade into her heart this day."

Kane's head snaps up and he looks at each of us as if trying to ascertain if that is correct information. I hold out my arms to him. "It's true, we're all family now."

He moves forward, his wings trembling. "I am truly accepted as well?"

I grab the front of his uniform and pull him down for a kiss. He seems like a guy who has never been kissed, so I go slow. I feel Hero at my back. Their wings come out to slip around me and it feels amazing to be between them. Hero's mouth lands on the back of my bare neck and he slips the straps from my shoulders and trails kisses down.

They both smell amazing, but nothing like what Hero did that first night.

The door slides open again and Hatch stalks in. "I got a message from Pern to come home at once. I'm glad I took his message seriously. It seems our prospective queen is handing out kisses."

I can tell by his tone that he's trying to be funny. I'm too aroused to be all that amused. "You look like crap. What the hell happened?"

Tossing aside some kind of utility belt he had slung over his shoulder, he begins moving forward. "Warriors fight. It's what we do. Fighting is dangerous, difficult and dirty work, my queen." As Kane and Hero move back slightly, his eyes slide over me from head to toe. His intake of breath is audible. "You look much better in that gown than I dared to imagine a queen would when I bought it. If you are giving out kisses, I want mine."

He clearly saw more action than Kane because he's still all ramped up from the adrenaline rush or whatever the Draconian equivalent is. "You get kisses after you shower."

"I want kisses now."

The two males at my side tense and it gives me an idea. Smoothing my hands down my perfectly respectable new dress, I purr, "I'd love to give you a kiss, maybe more than one. But I need you to keep your hands to yourself."

Hatch's rough voice answers as expected. "A kiss and a challenge it is then, my demanding queen."

I walk over to him and he crams his hands into his uniform pockets. I didn't even know uniforms had pockets because mine doesn't. I run one finger down the seam of his uniform, not keen on leaning in to kiss him. It has a big splotch of blood on the side and another of something bright orange. I pull the magnetic seam open and slide it back off his shoulders. It bunches around his waist, locking his hands into his pockets. I reach one hand up around his neck to pull him down for a kiss. He come with absolutely no resistance.

My hands roam over his large muscular chest as we kiss over and over again. When he parts his lips I slip my tongue into his mouth. He makes a desperate needy sound in the back of his throat. When I pull back I can see a kind of aggressive lust that should scare me but it doesn't. When he speaks, his voice is breathless. "Thank you, my queen, for gifting me with a human kiss. I have always wished to experience one." He means a long drawn out one, with tongues and all.

Stepping back, I run one finger over his magnificent abs. "If you run along and have a nice shower, I'll let you be in charge the first five microns when you return. We'll all do anything you want." The look that jumps onto his face is hard to identify. It makes me anxious, thrilled and everything in between.

Turning, I look at Kane's less messy but still soiled uniform. "You get the same deal if you want."

Kane sprints past Hatch who's still trying to get his hands untangled. The moment he realizes Kane is trying to get to the mister first he goes running after him. I stand there watching the two of them, thinking they are going to be smart enough to take turns when they get to the door. But of course they don't because they both want to be first. I turn my back while they're both stuck in the doorframe jostling to get the other one to pull back.

The corners of Hero's lips turn up. "What is my prize for maintaining love making readiness?"

I know he's joking but now I'm not. I go to my knees in front of him, working the seam of his uniform open and pulling it back off his shoulders and down as we go. When his thick cock pops free, I take it in my hands. The jostling at the door stops, so I assume they sorted out a pecking order for showering.

Hero looks down at me and his nostrils flare. "What do you do, my queen?"

"I'm rewarding my male because he makes me feel beautiful and desired." Without waiting, I lean over and lick the crown of his cock. He sucks in a stuttering breath and slides his legs apart. His tail drifts through the slit in the side of my gown and goes immediately to my girlie bits. I can tell the exact moment he discovers I have no underthings on. His eyes go wide and his lip peels back to reveal one fang.

I cover the head of his cock with my open mouth and take as much of him as I can. The more I use my tongue and suck, the more noises he makes. I'm about a hundred percent sure he's never even thought of getting oral sex. I love knowing that I'm blowing his mind. While the others are showering, this is just my time alone with my first, my protector, my love. I hate the thought of playing favorites, but Hero might be my favorite. I feel a little guilty about that, so I suck harder. He smells and tastes really nice, making me want to use my tongue more.

I remember he's carrying my young and gently caress the area right in front of his hip. I feel a small hand-sized swell. Hero loses it. He's rocking himself in and out of my mouth in short shallow strokes. He's trying to talk but the words are coming out all mangled and strange. He's all kinds of cute until he shoots his load in my mouth. I swallow quickly and the motion just seems to inflame him more. The weird thing is he stops coming before I'm done tasting him.

He pulls me up and holds me against his huge chest. When he turns to take me to the sleeping room, I see two stunned clan members still stuck in the doorway. I almost laugh. These men are too much sometimes. They aren't even trying to leave the room anymore. Jax is also standing just inside the door, gaping at us. He's apparently showered and donned a clean uniform before leaving medical because he's immaculate.

Hero roars at Hatch and Kane, "Move. Our queen needs to be pleasured and I am but one male."

Jax begins to move towards our sleeping room. "Yes, do move. At least one member of our clade is ready to pleasure our queen." He preens a bit as he leads the way to the huge clan sized bed. Hatch and Kane are on the move again but I pay them no mind in favor of watching Jax take off his uniform. When he turns, his wings flare out and his head comes up. He's standing so still I begin to wonder if he even wants to have any sexy fun.

He finally frowns. "If I weren't taking the suppressor my mating scent would be swamping you. I'm at a disadvantage at the moment so bear that in mind during your inspection."

I gesture for him to come to me. "Human women don't inspect their males for flaws. I forgot that was a thing with Draconians."

Moving forward with grace I've never seen in one of their kind, he asks curiously, "If you do not inspect your males for obvious flaws, how do you know they're fit for breeding?"

"Well, if they're walking, talking and have a hard-on that makes them fit for breeding." Looking down, I notice he doesn't quite have an erection. It's more like a chubby half-erection. "Would you be waiting for permission to get hard, perchance?"

He nods, his expression tense. "It is much more difficult to wait for approval than I thought it would be."

I look him in the eye so I'm sure he understands. "Human women love erections. Getting hard spontaneously around your own queen is a mark of respect. It means you find her attractive and wish to mate."

His cock springs to attention in the blink of an eye. He drops down on the bed beside me and falls back with a sigh. His wings are spread out and one is curled up resting against my hip. His cock is standing straight up and for such a small man, his cock is ginormous. "That is such a relief. I don't know how breeders keep from getting hard without permission. It's painfully difficult. I even thought about all the grossest things I could remember. Nothing helped when I was watching you pleasure Hero with your mouth."

"You liked that, did you?"

As if remembering himself, he bolts up. "Sorry, I didn't mean to act casual during..."

I jump on him and shove him onto his back. I'm still fully clothed and he's totally naked. Something about that turns me on. I see his eyes are totally zeroed in on my breasts. His hot gaze is making me think really naughty thoughts. I slip off the straps of my gown and bend forward to kiss him. He's all eager lips and sharp fangs. We'll have to work on kissing properly later because his straining cock is poking me in the stomach. I slide back and onto my knees, pulling him up as well. His cock is leaking and I use it to lube him all the way down. Rather than putting him in my mouth, I place his cock between my breasts and use my hands to smash him between my bountiful globes. I almost snort a laugh at how easily I can work that silly word into almost any situation.

When I look up to see if Jax is okay with this, his face is nothing short of astounded. He points to where our bodies are joined and points out excitedly, "My cock is between your breasts."

"You approve?"

"I do. If you move, I will make a gigantic mess on you. I just thought you should know." Jax is so sweet and innocent, I can hardly stand not being able to kiss him and fuck him with my breasts all at the same time. Then I remember those fangs and decide I've got the better end of the deal for now.

Hatch's voice sounds from the side. "I think you are meant to shower your queen with your seed. She wishes it."

Jax makes a sound of disbelief. "This is allowed? I wish it as well."

I look him in the eyes and say, "Try not to come. It's a game to see how long you last."

"This is my very first love game. I'm glad it is a challenging one."

I slowly move up and down and he jerks. "Your skin is so soft, like nothing I have ever felt."

Deciding to up the game, I tilt my head down and lick the head of his cock each time I pull back. Jax is so damn easy to please that it breaks my heart. He's not even getting sex and he's having the time of his life. Of course, as obsessed with breasts as these guys are, maybe this is a level of erotic I'm not seeing.

He shakes his head. "I'm not going to last."

"This isn't the only time you'll get to do this. We can practice every day until you can last a really long time."

His head snaps down to look me in the eyes. "Every day?"

When I nod, his cock twitches and I know he's going to go off. I grab him with both hands and give him a good hard stroke as I lean away. A growl to my right tells me his seed probably hit someone. Glancing back, I see Hatch wiping at his chest with a uniform. Jax drops back onto the bed, totally spent. As strong arms grasp me from behind, I see

Jax roll away and grab for a hydration pack across the bed. He's clearly making room for the ones who haven't had sex yet, like me.

Hatch stands me on the bed and backs away as I turn around. Talk about being put on a pedestal. For the first time I feel like a queen with her harem of sexy males. All of them are naked. Hero is sitting across the room watching me as he languidly strokes his ginormous cock. He looks happy and mostly sated. Jax is leaning against the side wall, sipping a hydration packet. His cock is at half mass but he seems to not even notice. Now Hatch and Kane are a different matter. They're looking needy and eager.

Hatch's voice surprises me. He sounds rough and almost animalistic. "Take off the gown, my beautiful queen. We wish to look our fill."

He's not asking. He's demanding. I remember the deal about him being in charge when he got out of the shower. Although my upper torso is on full display, that's not enough for them. I guess this is part of what separates talkers from doers. Hooking my thumbs into the stretchy waist of the gown, I slide it down and kick it off the bed.

Hatch sneaks a glance at Hero. "You're right, she does have pale curls that match her hair."

Hero nods, still slowly stroking that cock. "She tastes better than the finest food or drink. Nothing compares to the taste of our queen."

Hatch motions to the others. "Come, we will all taste. Show us, Hero."

It hits me that Hatch wants Hero to show them how to handle my body, since he's the only one that has touched me intimately. That's kind of sweet.

Hero stands and walks over with his cock bobbing. He lifts me, placing one knee on either of his muscular shoulders and spreads me open over his face. I have to grasp his horns to keep my balance. He pulls me open a little more and his tongue comes out to run through my folds. When he hits my clit, I'm so wound up from all the foreplay, I go off almost immediately. The orgasm is delightful but I feel so empty.

Hatch grasps me around the waist and turns me around in Hero's arms. He holds one bent leg in each hand and the small of my back is against his face. Jax moves forward and runs his fingers through my pubic hair. "I saw this on the females in the medical bay but never dared to touch. You are soft and petable here."

Hatch's rough voice growls, "Taste or leave, Jax."

He lowers his mouth to my mound, and when he pushes his tongue into my core, I almost scream. He licks me there, thrusting his tongue in and out. He finds my g-spot and stays with it until I'm shaking his horns and moaning his name. When my legs shake and I explode on his tongue he laps all the quicker, as if trying to make sure none gets away.

The hot possessive look on his face when he pulls back tells me he's just getting started. Before long he's going to be just as hot for me as the rest of my clan. Something about seeing Jax come into his own sexually almost makes me come again.

Now it's just down to Kane and Hatch again. Hero lays me on the bed on my front and pulls my hips up into the air.

Two strong hands lift me up slightly and a hot mouth attacks my tender flesh with yet another sensual assault. I realize the mouth on me is Kane when Hatch crawls onto the bed and presents his cock for me to suck. The thing is, I want him this way. I never thought I'd love something like this in a million years. But truth be told, I fucking love it.

I test how he tastes on my tongue and discover he's just as delicious as Hero. He tastes a bit like plums. This man risked his life for me today and he's been nothing but nice and accommodating. His green skin has a pattern almost like camouflage and his tail is flicking back and forth excitedly. To me he's one of the most handsome men I've ever met. Why wouldn't I want him?

I quiet all the internal crap and try to shove aside the pleasure Kane is giving and concentrate on sucking Hatch's cock like he deserves. We're all getting pleasure tonight and I'm getting much more than my share. I swirl my tongue around the tip and suck for all I'm worth, hollowing out my cheeks in an effort to show him how much I care about his needs.

His hand fists in my hair and for one brief moment I know fear. He only rocks back and forth like Hero did. I can't use both hands on him because I've got one holding myself up.

Suddenly, Kane hits my clit and I pull off Hatch long enough to scream his name. Hatch pulls me up flush with his body and then lays me back down facing him. My clit is throbbing like nobody's business. All I can think about is having Hatch's cock inside my body. Looking him in the eyes, I slowly spread my legs. Our clan leader is a really smart guy. He doesn't need to be told twice. Dropping down with one hand near my shoulder, he brings his face down to mine. "Say it."

At first I'm confused. Then it dawns on me that he wants me to say it's okay to have full-on sex. I don't know what gets into me but I want him to think of me as more than just a hole to fuck. I want him to see me as smart, sexy and funny so I say what comes to mind. "You've got a really nice cock there. I've a nice place to put it if you're interested in having a little fun."

His expression lights up and he quips, "I thought you'd never ask."

When he comes down on top of me, all I want in the world is to have full-on sex one time tonight, with him. My hands come up to smooth the bruises on his face. He was injured protecting me and everyone else on this ship. "You're a hero too. Too bad the name is taken."

His hand comes up to skate over the side of my face. "You are all we could ever hope for in a queen. I promise that you will never regret taking us to you."

I feel him slowly impaling me with his cock. Rather than rocking, he pushes slowly forward, making me take all of his endowment. I wiggle, trying to accept all that he's insisting upon giving me. I love the way he fills me and the intense look on his face while he's doing it. He pauses when he's all the way in and then with a slight smirk he pulls out and fills me again, a little faster. His hips work back and forth, building to the most exquisite orgasm I've ever had. His chest brushes against me and his tail is probing places it shouldn't but I don't complain. He shifts his hips and suddenly he's hitting everywhere at once. When he leans down to say absolutely dirty stuff in my ear, I finally lose control and come. When I tighten down around his cock, his rhythm breaks and he empties deep inside me. He stays in place for a bit and we just catch our breath. He whispers sweet things to me about his love and how they're going to make sure I'm never feeling lonely or unloved for the rest of my life. He's about the sweetest man I've ever met. Maybe he's my favorite.

When Hatch pulls back, I sit up and look around. Hero is back in his chair with a flaccid cock. I assume he stroked himself off to the sight of Hatch and I having sex, which is fine by me. Jax is lounging on what appears to be a trunk with a bunch of pillows stacked on it. His cock is standing fully erect but he's all smiles and actually waves at me. I smile at him but don't wave back, cause that's just weird.

Kane is standing patiently by and I realize that I'm kind of beat and still have one clan member to go. Maybe four really is too many. Instead of making a move to have sex with me, though, he carries me to the cleaning room. Yeah, I am kind of a mess but strangely enough I love smelling like my clan, at least in the confines of our own quarters.

Instead of a shower, he's run a bath. I honestly didn't know we even had a bath. Apparently, the contraption has glass-like panels that slide up from the floor creating a large square tube the size of the shower enclosure. My anxiety spikes a little because Kane is the one I've spent the least amount of time with.

I quickly learn he's the most accommodating. He lowers the lights, adds scented oil to our bath and sits me in the water before sliding in behind me. Looking over my shoulder, I murmur, "The only thing missing is romantic music."

Kane smiles down at me as he rubs oil onto his hands. "Draconians do not have music for mating, only for fighting. You would not find it relaxing, my queen."

When his hands begin massaging my back, I melt into his touch. "You're really good at making women happy."

"I should say so. It is what I spent my entire life learning to do." Something about his voice is off.

"Didn't you want to be a...a...what do you call males who take care of women. We call them spa attendants on Earth."

"I understand there was some misunderstanding about that when we first encountered your kind. You already know all males are either breeders or warriors. What most do not understand is that taking care of a Draconian queen requires many males. Only a small cross-section of the males actually get to breed for their queen."

Relaxing under his expert touch, I respond, "I did not know that."

"Obviously, my father was bred. I was not looking forward to being selected."

"If you don't want a queen why did you join our clan?"

His voice takes on a lighter tone. "I never wished for a queen until I met you. Bumping into you in the marketplace took my breath away."

Looking behind me again, I laugh. "Really? You seemed terrified to me."

"I was shocked to see such a lovely human where none were supposed to be. I tried to talk to you but no words came. I rallied my team to help me find you, and once we did, I was loath to leave off of guarding you. I believe Hatch noticed my growing obsession with you. He wished for his clade and offered me inclusion as well. I believe he thought you would accept them to get me. It's clear to my eyes that you accept me to get them."

I jerk forward and turn in the water to face him. "That's not true. You seemed really nice when I met you. It's just that Hero helped Trovena and kept her safe until help could arrive. I felt certain that if he could see her as a person he could see me as one too."

Skimming his hands over the top of the water he shakes

his head slightly. "You are a proper queen. Who would not see you as a person?"

I can't keep the shocked expression off my face. "Maybe all the assholes who thought it was okay to buy and sell me. The ones who kept me in a cage and often forgot to feed me definitely didn't see me as a person."

"There are some ignorant species that don't see anyone other than themselves as sentient. We get exhausted from dealing with them. I wish they would evolve already."

His words are profound and funny at the same time. It helps me let go of my anger. "I wish they would as well. It's lucky that you stumbled over me in the marketplace. If you hadn't I'd probably still be there."

Raising one hand to remove a strand of hair from my face, he murmurs, "I am glad you are here with us. You are a sweet queen who deserves a clade of males to look after her every need."

"What about you? Don't you deserve a female to look after all your needs?"

His expression turns serious. "I feel obligated to let you know that you are offering far more than we were expecting and vastly more than we would have settled for in terms of intimacy."

"Are you saying you don't want sex?"

"I would like sex very much. You should understand something first. Draconian females go into heat once a year. They fill their chamber with many males. Usually their primary breeder is a queen maker, but not always. They breed until her heat is over. The males who were not breeding directly with the queen are activated by the pheromones in the room."

"What are you saying?" I realize in an instant what he's telling me. "I might have gotten every single one of you with child tonight?" I smack my own forehead for not researching Draconian mating habits before trying to have sex with them. What in the hell am I going to do with dozens of kids?

Kane gently takes my hands in his. "Take a deep breath, my queen. Our clade leader decided to take a more practical approach to spawning for our family unit. When he realized that you had already chosen Hero, he had the rest of us take a suppressor. If he hadn't, our combined mating scents would have emptied out every being on this level, except the females who likely would have been beating down the door to get in."

At first I think he's joking and then I realize he's not. "Thank goodness. I don't want to end up fighting off every woman on this ship to keep my clade."

"We would not accept their attention, for we only wish you for our queen."

"That's real sweet of you to say. Now where were we on the having some sex stuff, cause I've never thought of myself as a quitter."

"Why don't you relax and rest your weary body. I will not press my cause with you tonight. I have been relieving my own needs for years and it would be an honor to do it one more time in favor of giving you time to rest."

"Wait. Are we talking about you stroking yourself off in front of me? That's something I wouldn't mind seeing."

He wrinkles his nose in an expression that seems like he might doubt my words.

"I'm serious about seeing if breeders can last as long as warriors."

His expression turns devious. "Those are words fit to provoke a fight. Breeders are better at everything to do with sex than regular warriors."

"Those are bold words. Wanna back them up with some action? If so I'm all in."

"You are teasing me with the one thing I most wish to experience."

"How about I give you a little kiss to help you decide?" Unsure why I'm baiting this breeder into having sex with me, I move forward and climb straight into his lap. Unlike Jax, this man knows exactly what he's doing. His wings spread out behind him and his tail comes up behind me, jerking me forward expectantly. I look up into his eyes and know all the way down to my soul this man was made for sex. I let him know what I'm thinking. "Hatch was right about you."

I don't even have to explain. This confident breeder knows exactly what I mean. He's hot and well trained to deliver pleasure. He spreads his legs and I know what this devious breeder is going to do before he does it. The tip of his tail comes up, spearing me. My breath catches at the sensation. Kane's leaned back like a conquering hero with both arms spread out along the bath. His dark eyes devour my naked form as he watches me squirm on his tail. When he hits my g-spot, I begin moving against him.

His expression is expectant and I know he's waiting for me to break. One more rub and the orgasm washes over me. He pulls his tail away too fast for my liking and I'm shocked when he brings it to my lips. "Taste what I risked my life to protect today, my beautiful queen."

Somehow this man has me in his thrall, but I'm not that far gone yet. When I shake my head, he laughs and pulls it back. I watch him lick it clean and decide that I want that tail in my mouth at some point. I mean, it's going to be nice and clean and the mood has to be right, but it's going to happen.

It occurs to me that these Draconians start out all subservient but if you give them an inch they'll take a mile. The sexy needy pricks really love to tease and pleasure their queens, I'll give them that.

He looks at me as though he's trying to decide what to do to me. I stand, step out of the water and turn so he can watch me dry off. I use nice long languid strokes with the soft cloth that's too large to be a washcloth and too small to be a towel. His gaze grows more heated by the moment. He slowly rises and hits the dryer without draining the water. I know this means he's eager to jump me, so I toss the cloth at him and take off running for the bed.

He's at my back before I can even get to the door, lifting me and carrying me into the sleeping room. The others are all on the bed at this point but they move back to make room. My anxiety ratchets up a notch. I'm in the bed with four men, men who consider me their wife. I panic and begin trying to crawl away. Kane's hands come down around my hips and he pulls me back and up until my back is pressed against his chest. "I can scent your fear, my queen. It is insulting to think that you still do not trust us not to harm you."

I look at the men around me and the others are a mixture of confused and angry. Hero's angry and since I don't want to give him the impression Kane did anything untoward to me, I explain myself. "When I first met you, I had this illogical fear of you flying off with me, tossing me back and forth in the air."

Hero is the one who speaks up. "We would never take such a risk with our one and only queen."

"I know that now. But something about you all being around me triggered that thought and all the fear came back."

Kane motions the others forward. "We need to acclimate you to being the center of our world. When you are surrounded by your males, you should feel safe and protected."

They all gather around me and I feel stupid for freaking out. Kane runs his nose down my neck and the other touch me with the intent to calm not arouse. Unfortunately, it's turning me on. I can tell the exact moment they realize what's going on because their touches turn bolder. Kane's hand cups my chin and he turns me sideways and takes my lips. Hands palm my breasts and toy with my nipples. Someone's fingers slip through my now slick again folds. I think it's Hero because he slides a finger inside me and then two.

When Kane breaks the kiss, the others move back. "I believe you lured me into sex just because you are too nice to leave me out."

Glancing back, I smile up at him. "I want you and I'm curious about having a breeder."

"Then a breeder you shall have, my queen."

I feel his tail moving forward but he moves me onto my hands and knees on the bed. I remember his mouth on me in this position. I don't want his mouth this time, because I'm already dripping wet for him. I don't have to say it, because he's intuitive. His cock moves to my core and then he begins to slide in. He's really well-endowed so it takes a breathtaking series of thrusts before he's seated fully inside me. I like the way he handles me. The others kind of dig their fingers in a bit, but Kane is really careful and uses the palms of his hands to move me back and forth. I realize he's got one hand turned up and the other down, so he can use his palms to both push and pull depending on the kind of stroke he's making.

I fall under his thrall, allowing him to do with me as he desires. When he's in deep, he pulls me back against his chest, making me think he's a natural cuddler. His hands cross over my stomach so he can move me up and down. When he starts thrusting it's all pleasure and no pain.

Just when I'm starting to get into it, his tail comes up. Did I say I was fascinated with that thing? It pokes around where our bodies join and I realize he's lubricating it. On a downward thrust, it moves between my legs and the blunt under bottom covers my clit. When it moves I let loose a throaty moan. It feels like the underside is covered in little suckers that gently tug at my sensitive nub.

It's all I can do not to scream as this breeder has his sexy way with me. At some point I realize that he's riding me hard until I'm about to explode and then dialing it back, making sure the orgasm is just out of reach. The first couple of times I love it. After that it starts making me mad. I whisper, "Don't tease me, babe."

He bites my neck before replying. "Tell me what you want, my queen. Command and I will obey."

"I want to come."

He continues, and the tip pressing against my clit presses firmer. "More," I whisper.

I get more but not enough. I make a sound of frustration. He moves me forward onto my hands and knees, and when he rides me it feels like he has two cocks, one in my body and the other one rubbing my clit. Cognitively I know it's his sexy-ass tail, but something gets messed up in my mind and I envision two cocks.

His hands come to my hips and he kicks up the energy, I can feel this man all the way into the back of my throat. I've never been so full or thought I could be without breaking apart. I feel every square inch of the slide and it's pure bliss.

My whole world narrows to what is going on between our legs. I won't last much longer.

Finally, his tail pulls back and slaps my clit. The pain and pleasure explode, setting off the most explosive orgasm I've ever had. He doesn't touch my clit again because if he did, I think I'd die. It's throbbing to the beat of his cock which is spasming in my channel. Instead it comes up to grasp my shoulder, locking me to him.

Only then do I realize he's wrapped my hair around one gigantic fist. I normally like a little light hair-pulling, so I'm sorry I was too far gone with the rest of his technique that I missed it.

When I calm, he jerks me back a couple of times to empty the last of his seed into my womb. It seems like something a breeder would do and it feels good, so I don't object. Looking over at the end of his tail still wrapped over my shoulder, I can smell myself on it. Sweet day in the morning, what the hell have I gotten myself into with these men.

When he flips me over and comes down on top of me, it's to kiss my neck and tell me how wonderful I am. His expression is awed and reverent. Wrapping my arms around him, I guess the sexy bastard has a soft side. It makes me like him more. Gazing up at him I can almost see this one becoming my favorite.

He smiles as if he can intuit my thoughts. "I think that whoever you have in your arms will be favored in that moment."

I jerk back slightly. "Are you a freakin' mind reader?"

A smile ghosts across his face. "Breeders are intuitive, my queen. If we could read minds our training wouldn't take twenty years."

The others crawl forward and we are a tangle of bodies lying every which way, with me in the middle. I wonder if any woman ever had it so good. There was no jealousy, arguing or discord, just four men looking for a little sexy fun. I cuddle up to Kane's chest with Hero at my back, thinking that maybe I can actually do this. More importantly, I want to do this, have a clan instead of one man. These men are all sweet, loving and respectful. They're good all the way down to their cores and I would miss the others if I had to pick just one. Lucky for me, I don't have to choose. I can fall hopelessly into the happily ever after they are offering with open arms.

LATISHA

WE'RE ALL IN CROVAN'S SHUTTLE FOR A VISIT TO Earth. Even Trovena came along for the day. Her young are old enough to stay in the hatchery, so it ought to be fun to see how that works out.

"You are not permitted to look at me, Sonarian."

Trovena lifts her head and stares at Crovan even harder. "You are not much to look at, but no male gives me orders."

"You are aboard my ship, so you will follow my orders."

Trovena snorts a laugh. "You have no power over me, lawman. I'll do as I like."

They are driving Hatch crazy, so I call for Trovena to come over and sit with me. "I have the first visual on my underground city, Trovena. Would you like to see?"

She pounces over and puts one gigantic paw in my lap and the other on the control panel. We hear Crovan complain, "Don't leave claw marks on my equipment."

Trovena reaches over with one claw to make a scrape down the side of his shiny state of the art console and I grab her claw. She wheezes a laugh. "It would blend in with all the other scratches. He'd never know."

"Let's not piss him off until we find out what my mother had to trade him to find me."

"Remember the story you told of the old man who spun silk?"

I stifle a laugh. "It wasn't her firstborn. That was me and I'm already mated."

Her snout goes up in the air. "For which you can thank me."

I give her a quick hug, just like old times. "Yeah, I'll give you credit for that one. It's a good thing they followed me, cause they saved your life and the lives of all your young."

Her face morphs into an unreadable expression and she turns to look at Hatch. Her voice turns from playful to serious in a heartbeat. "I am grateful for what I have and think often upon what I have lost. Your clan will always be in my prayers for their service to me and mine."

"I'm not sure how we ended up in the deep end of the conversation but you know we all love you and your little ones. You'll always have a place with us, Trovena."

Her large paw comes out and she playfully bats me in the face. "I know this already." She preens a bit and then slinks away to aggravate Crovan some more.

I rub my cheek. It feels warm but doesn't sting too much. Trovena has seen the males slapping each other on the backs and I know that's where the paw in the face came from. She's mimicking their cultural behavior as best she can to fit in. All I can say is, it's a good thing her claws were retracted.

Crovan's irritated voice rises. "Leave that alone, Trovena. It houses all my personal mental images."

I twirl my chair around. "Oh, that sounds interesting."

Trovena's paw immediately comes up to the roller ball imbedded in the console and gives it a spin. We all freeze in our seats as mental images get blasted into our minds of my family. Crovan is lying in a grassy field with my mother's head resting in his lap. She's smiling up at him. My brothers and sisters are all playing nearby. My hands tighten on the chair arm when I realize that I'm playing there as well. Everything looks just like it did when I was a child. It is an image of Earth before the fall and it's so realistic that it brings tears to my eyes. Suddenly, the images snap shut in my mind.

I hear Crovan and Trovena arguing; only now Corvan has the ball in his hand. "You have no right to go through my personal thoughts."

The peacekeeper is in love with my mother and inventing idyllic scenarios in his mind of them together. My heart skips a beat and a chill crawls right up my spine because I now know what my mother traded. The bastard made her sign a contract that she'd belong to him. I'm holding onto the arm rests so tightly my knuckles go white. I want to scream the walls down.

Hatch is at my side in an instant. "Calm yourself, my queen. We will work this out. I promise you that we will not abandon your mother to this peacekeeper."

His voice is low and earnest. "We have resources and can make a trade if need be." Suddenly, all the jewels and fancy dresses in the world can't fix this situation. I wish I could go back all those years ago and rethink signing up for the galactic brides program. Sure, I was able to get a nice chunk of change for my family but in the end everything went sideways and my mother sacrificed herself to get me back.

Her words come back to me full force. *"Come home, Latisha. It's the only way."* That can only mean she needs me to sign up for the brides program again to earn money.

That doesn't make sense. The truth hits me like a ton of bricks. She wants me to take my younger siblings because she has to go with Corvan. He must not have wanted a bunch of teens hanging around. In his fantasy we were all children. He wants little ones, not people who are practically adults.

Shame and self-doubt fill my head for the first time. Maybe all my happiness isn't meant to last. All this time Hatch has been talking but I zoned out on him. He's now looking at me expectantly and I nod, like I know what in the flip he said. I just can't handle hearing it all again right now.

When the shuttle lands I rush to the door. My mother and siblings are waiting for us. I run down the ramp and right into their arms. I'm wearing a plain gown and no jewelry because it would be seen as bragging on Earth. They still look at me with wide eyes.

My mother puts her hands on my shoulders and stands back a bit. "Let me look at you, girl. You look so nice and well cared for."

I introduce each of my clan in turn and she seems more impressed than appalled that I have four husbands. They all do their kneeling thing and it freaks her out a bit but I push past that. She looks me in the eyes and asks the one question I knew she would. "Are you truly happy, dear?"

I can't keep the smile off my face as I remember the last three months. We've argued, fought, made up, made love and played together. "I'm more happy now than I've ever been in my life."

"I'm so glad. You can't know how happy I am to see you again."

Her eyes drift over my shoulder as Corvan stomps down the ramp, still carrying his ball of fantasies.

"Are you alright? Tell me what's going on."

My mother straightens, clearly steeling herself for what is to come.

Corvan comes to stand face-to-face with her. "I have quested as you asked and fulfilled every task you have demanded of me. Will you now fulfill your end of the bargain?"

She smiles at him, just like she did in his fantasy. "It would be an honor and a pleasure."

My gaze flies back and forth between the two of them. She's way too satisfied with her end of the bargain. That must mean she didn't sacrifice herself. Relief courses through my body.

He uses his com device to bring up a contract. It's all in Arobian so I can't read it. She signs off on it. There is already another signature. I assume it's his. They stand staring at each other for a long moment. Just when I think she's going to turn and leave, she flings herself into his arms instead. Instead of kissing, they rub foreheads. His third eye glows and encases them in a little glowing bubble.

I step back as the reality of her situation slams home. She's in love with him and used that to get him to track me down. I don't know whether to be angry or proud. My mother finally found herself an alien mate. If all that glowing is really their version of kissing then I'm gonna say she really likes him.

My oldest sister meanders over with the others following. I try not to watch our mom loving on the peacekeeper but it's hard not to notice cause they seem to be having a moment. "Do they do that often?"

"Every chance they get. It's called psy-bonding and it's supposedly the greatest things since wireless."

I laugh at her old-fashioned saying. Looking her over, I can't help but notice she's looking pretty grown up for seventeen. "Stephanie, would you like to meet my husbands?"

She rolls her eyes, since she already met them when I introduced them a bit ago. I was just trying to stir up some conversation cause things are hitting the awkward stage. "Hard pass. I'm about all aliened out for a while."

Trovena's voice is growly. "Tell the peacekeeper to stop accosting your mother." When I look over, I see she has my youngest brother between her paws and is licking his hair. He's giggling and trying to get away.

Stephanie shrugs. "You can interrupt them if you want but I wouldn't. It's hard to tell what they're thinking about and you might end up seeing something you regret."

Kane is trying to get little Donnie away from Trovena and I'm not sure how to explain to her but I give it a try. "Trovena isn't a pet. She's a person."

"I could tell because of the licking."

"About that. She just had children and, well, now she has a propensity to groom everyone."

"Keep her away from my hair, will ya?"

"You don't seem all that fazed by strange alien breeds these days, Steph." Kicking my foot through the dust on the ground I ask, "What's been going on around here that you're not freaking out?"

She waves one delicate hand towards the sky. "We've seen about everything you can imagine. Your Sonarian friend isn't even the first one of her kind I've seen. Ships keep coming and going, all day long every day. There isn't much we haven't seen."

I wave Hero over. "My sister wants a bird's eye view of this area. Would you mind helping her out with that?"

"As you wish, my queen." Bending swiftly, he picks her up and they're airborne within moments. Her eyes are huge but she's got a gigantic smile on her face. I guess I still have a surprise or two up my sleeve.

Donnie runs over. "Wanna ride." Hatch grins, because now I've started something that's going to keep my four hunky mates busy for the foreseeable future. Yeah, this is going to get fun.

———

READY FOR MORE SEXY Draconian adventures? Read Alien Savage's Stolen Bride (Draconian Warriors Book 7) now!

Akes – Draconian god of hunting, war and violence. He is the consort to Entares, the benevolent goddess worshiped by Draconian males.

Antar – Right (Lutar is left.)

Arobian – Milky white tall aliens with small mouths and telepathic third eye.

Avada – Small carrot-like vegetable that is seasoned and wrapped in a dry leaf.

Challenge – Draconian queens settle disagreements and property disputes by challenging one another in single combat. It is usually a battle to the death.

Clade – Group of Draconians who are descended from a common set of genetic code. Can also be a set of Draconian males who come together to claim a queen.

Dark Star – Another term for blackhole.

Doma – Type of Draconian flatbread.

Dracon Two – The nickname the second wave of Draconian warriors gave their new home world. Dracon Two's real name is Onello. It is located in Naxis space. The planet was originally named by

Queen Cassandra after a Greek god. It was unofficially renamed Dracon Two because the name their new queen chose is very near the word for feces in the Draconian tongue.

Draconian - Species created by mixing dragon DNA with humanoid DNA. There are many family lines with unique strengths and weaknesses.

Entares – Draconian goddess of beauty, peace and joy. The males worship her as she represents their desire for females to show kindness and respect to them for their many sacrifices, rather than the harsh treatment they normally receive.

Entaza – Dish eaten with the living larva still wiggling in the dish. Common food in Exion space.

Exion – Vast Sector of space encompassing the Draconian home world. Exion is ruled by a race of ruthless females bent on conquest and power.

Hatching – Draconian method of reproduction by which warriors conceive and carry eggs.

Hatchling – Noun: Child. Males hatch many times during their lifetimes.

Hatch Mate – Refers to only the children hatched during the same cycle of breeding.

Lankean – Word that means beloved or loved ones.

Laser Pistol – A weapon used in battles and self-defense which uses power packs to fire short laser bursts.

Lunar – Equivalent of a complete phase of the primary moon traveling around Dracon One. This is a standard unit of measurement used by many spacefaring species, even when not on their home planets.

Lutar - Left. (Antar is Right)

Maradox – Queen Ravonda's ship, which was boarded and taken by Queen Cassandra and Mathadar.

Moltan – Malevolent aliens who attack and destroy other vessels.

Naxis – Vast sector of space encompassing five galaxies, including the Milky Way.

Obsidian – The name of a Draconian ship.

Parsec – Unit of distance. Used mostly in determining distance in space.

Parthenogenesis – Draconians males undergo parthenogenesis when exposed to a female's pheromones. It results in them incubating eggs in their bodies which are released into specially designed incubators.

Phase Grenade – Device that sticks to the hull of a ship and disables their weapons.

Revidian – The word used by Draconians to denote a warrior performing oral sex on a queen.

Scion – A word used for offspring, no matter the age.

Solar Revolution – Equivalent of a complete revolution of Dracon One around its sun. This is a standard unit of measurement used by many spacefaring species, even when not on their home planets.

Sonarian – Feline person that speaks. Has a strange sense of humor.

Strador Five – Planet populated by amphibians who discovered Earth and decided to abduct human women to sell on the open market.

Strovian – Race of warriors who are at peace with the Draconians in the Naxis sector.

Tarken – Powerfully addictive drug used by queens in the Exion.

Takadon – The Draconian word for a male who is chosen to be the queen's primary breeder. He is to stay at her side constantly and is her protector.

Taladar – Species who initiated a trade agreement with

Earth to exchange much-needed food and other supplies for human brides.

Tankea – Draconian word meaning love between a parent and child or between siblings.

Unders – Anything worn under one's uniform or regular clothing.

Tricon – Unit of thickness.

Utaka Larva – Pupa stage of growth for a tiny colorful flying creature the Draconians keep for pets.

Vithacan – Symbionts that attach themselves to other creatures and survive off their emotional energy. Soul suckers is a disrespectful term for their race.

Zelerians – Race of squid-like creatures with few humanoid features.

JUNO WELLS

SEXY SCI-FI ROMANCE AUTHOR

## SUBSCRIBE TO JUNO WELL'S MAILING LIST

Are you interested in getting the latest updates from Juno
Wells?

CLICK HERE TO SUBSCRIBE

## ABOUT THE AUTHOR

Juno Wells grew up on Florida's Space Coast, watching the shuttles take off from Cape Canaveral. When she hit college, her childhood fantasies about space travel turned highly romantic. Now her mind reels with space adventures of fantastic alien lords in distant galaxies, and the earth women they love.

Wells' stories explore the complex, sensual relationships between inhabitants of different star systems. There are always happy endings just as there is always a new world to explore.

Her work is exclusive to Amazon, so read as much as you like with Kindle Unlimited.